BOOKS BY TIM MCBAIN & L.T. VARGUS
The Violet Darger series
The Victor Loshak series
The Scattered and the Dead series
The Awake in the Dark series
Casting Shadows Everywhere
The Clowns

CASTING SHADOWS EVERYWHERE

L.T. VARGUS
TIM MCBAIN

CASTING
SHADOWS
EVERYWHERE

CASTING SHADOWS EVERYWHERE

CHAPTER 1

KILLING SOMEONE IS A LOT harder than you'd imagine. Physically harder, I mean. On TV a guy strangles someone for like five seconds and the body slumps to the ground in a heap of dead just like that. In real life, it takes so long you wouldn't believe it.

See, I saw someone get strangled once when I was nine.

I milled around outside of this Dairy Queen on Park Street on the way home from school. Out of nowhere, Tony Vasser walked up and kicked me in the balls. He was this 13-year-old shithead from the trailer park around the corner from my house, and he absolutely goddamn delighted in torturing the younger kids in the neighborhood. Such as me.

One minute I'm minding my own business, doing pretend kick flips and pop shove-its off this picnic table, and the next thing I know, I'm rolling in the grass clutching my crotch.

Anyway, what Tony didn't know was that my cousin Nick was watching the whole thing from the parking lot. Nick was seventeen and even meaner than Tony. Not to me, I mean, but you know…

So Tony's mouth gaped with laughter. He's one of those slack-jawed people who always smile with their mouth wide open. All I could see was a row of top teeth hanging over a pink cavern that stretched back into blackness. Even in his school picture he smiled like that. Wide open mouth. It's a dim look.

Mouth breather?

Absolutely.

Anyway, his mouth still drooped into an open pit when Nick grabbed him by the shoulder and slapped him across the face. Open hand. He didn't say anything. He didn't even take the Winston out of the corner of his mouth. He just slapped. And it was loud as hell.

I remember that seemed pretty funny at first. I mean, I was still buckled over at the waist, hunched over a sack full of extreme ball pain. Obviously, I didn't mind seeing Tony get blindsided or whatever. But there's also something so disrespectful about a man slapping another man like that. Dismissive. It's almost worse than getting punched in a weird way, you know? Someone has to respect you as a threat enough to punch you. A slap is all contempt.

But then Nick's hands latched around Tony's throat and squeezed. And it didn't seem as funny anymore. Tony's mouth stayed as wide open as ever, but his expression changed from happy to pants-shitting scared.

Nick had this look in his eyes. Like a hawk. Not like he was enjoying it or anything. Just that fierce look like a big mean bird that doesn't feel anything beyond the aggression necessary to survive. Like he could swoop out of the sky and kill if he needed to. No mushy feelings.

Smoke twirled off the end of his cigarette into his eye, so he squinted harder on one side than the other. It almost made his face look incongruent and scarier. Like some messed up freak like Sloth from *The Goonies* or something.

He squeezed until the kid's face turned a dark red like wine, and then he squeezed harder as it faded from purple to a pale blue. It finally went gray like the ash on the tip of a cigarette.

2

Tony's eyes bulged. His mouth moved like he was trying to scream. His fingernails scraped at Nick's arms, but it was useless.

I had to pee. I remember that. And I wanted to tell Nick to stop, you know? To leave him alone and whatever. But I froze up. I didn't say a word. Didn't even move. Just stood there watching.

And that is me in a lot of ways. I freeze.

It is who I am.

This choking went on for what seemed like forever. A good two minutes, if not more, and believe me, two minutes is suddenly a goddamn eternity when you're watching someone get strangled to death.

And I was scared. Not of Nick, I mean. Just scared 'cause of how Tony looked all gray, and I knew that this was forever. That at this second in time I could still try to do something, but once it passed I couldn't take any of it back. No one could.

I didn't say anything, of course. Did I already mention the freezing? 'Cause yeah. That.

It wasn't so long before the shock in Tony's expression faded. He dropped to his knees, and his eyes drooped closed.

Nick squeezed for a few more seconds even after the body went limp. Then he kind of leaned the kid up against the cinder block wall of the Dairy Queen.

We stood looking down on the body in silence. The limp neck tilted his chin down onto his chest. It was so still there. The whole world was motionless.

Then Tony's torso spasmed. The wind sucked back into his lungs with a creaky gasping sound like sliding open some dried out dresser drawer. His face went back through the progression of colors in reverse.

Nick laughed. He laughed even harder when he saw how scared I looked. I thought Tony was dead for sure.

Instead, he stirred and coughed. His shithead eyes opened.

"Choked your ass out," Nick said and spat on the ground.

Tony tried to say something, but his voice sounded all scratchy, and I couldn't understand him. Nick started laughing again.

Then he went and got ice cream cones for him and me. I got vanilla dipped in chocolate.

♦   ♦   ♦

Holy shit. I just reread that first entry. If anyone ever reads this, they're going to think I'm a goddamn weirdo. But if you were there... I don't know.

My point was that it must take for-goddamn-ever to actually strangle someone to death. I just Googled it. Dude, that shit can take up to ten minutes. Can you imagine strangling someone for ten minutes? Unbelievable. I guess it's pretty common for people's hands to cramp up before they can actually kill the person, too, so they have to, like, stop and massage their hands before they go back and re-strangle 'em. What a nightmare.

Anyway, I was kind of wondering if I subconsciously started right out talking about Nick 'cause I want people to think that I am like him. Not that anyone will read this, of course, but the audience in my head, I guess. We're all the main character in our own heads, right?

The truth is that I am nothing like him. Nick, I mean. I am

the one who froze up. The one that will never get the girl. The one that wet the bed up until the age of fourteen. The one who gets picked on and pushed around. I mean, come on. Nobody would fuck with Nick.

♦　♦　♦

So I hung out with Nick today. It'd been a couple years since I'd seen him. My mom doesn't want me around him anymore since he got arrested for stealing a twelve-pack of Budweiser from a 7-11 a few years ago. Spent three months in the county jail and lived out of state for a while after that. I guess now he's a "bad influence."

Whatever. What Mom doesn't know I could just about squeeze into the Grand Canyon.

So Nick is 24, and he has his own apartment in town now. Well, he has this roommate, Donnie, so they share the place. The point is, there are no adults or parents or whatever. It's rad. I mean, the place is a dump, but you know...

Mostly I sat on the floor watching Nick and Donnie play Playstation. Donnie told some hilarious stories.

"Then there was the time I tried to shit off the bridge. You know that overpass that goes over West Street? I squatted off the edge of that. Tryin' to flop a sloppy deuce on some unsuspecting Buick Skylark or something, you know?"

Donnie tilted back his head and poured most of the contents of a can of Wild Cherry Pepsi down his throat.

"I missed," Donnie said and then burped.

"The shit, I mean. My shit missed the car. I didn't have the push I thought I would, so it smacked the road way the hell after the car had already passed," he said, shaking his head.

He had a wistful look in his eyes like he was still disappointed to this day.

"Loudest slap I ever heard, though. Like my turd was belly-smacking West Street."

See? Hilarious.

"Somehow the cops showed up pretty much immediately, and I had to run like hell with my pants half off."

He turned the Pepsi can upside down and shook the last few drops of high fructose corn syrup into his mouth before tossing the can in the general direction of the kitchen.

"Now if you'll excuse me, gentlemen, I gotta make a run for the border."

"You work tonight?" Nick said.

"Indeed," Donnie said. "I'm lookin' at eight hours of repeating this motion."

Donnie stood up and pantomimed something with his hands that looked sort of like a shotgun. He squeezed the trigger over and over and swung the barrel of the invisible firearm left and right.

"What's that?" I said.

Donnie looked down at his hands and then back at me.

"It's my gun," he said.

"Your Taco Bell gun?" I said.

"It's my sour cream gun."

I felt my eyebrows stretch as high as they could.

"Sour cream gun?"

Donnie nodded.

"It's like a caulk gun that splooges just the right amount of sour cream onto each Burrito Supreme," he said.

6

He did another series of hand movements, maybe like he was loading a second gun.

"And this here is my Guacamole Glock."

"Glock-amole?" Nick said.

Donnie just grinned. He aimed both guns at me and motioned like he was firing them.

"Is there a refried bean gun?" I said.

Donnie chortled.

"Oh, lord no. The beans get made in a giant stainless steel sink. We spray boiling water into this bean powder and then bam! Sink full of refried beans."

He holstered his condiment weapons before continuing.

"It's all very scientific over there at Taco Bell. We weigh each bag of food before we give it out to ensure that every chalupa and double decker taco has been crafted to precise corporate specifications."

So after Donnie left, it was just me and Nick. We sat on a couple of disintegrating La-Z-Boys, one gray and the other light green, relics of some upper-middle-class den circa 1986. Donnie had found the pair on the side of the road. The recliners had roaches in them that had miraculously died out without becoming a bigger problem in their apartment. One of the few perks of never having any food, I guess.

Without Donnie there for comic relief, the conversation dried up some. We played video games in relative silence for fifteen minutes before Nick spoke up.

"Did you hear about the stiff they found above Broad Street?" Nick said.

My mind tried to process this sentence and failed.

"Stiff?" I said.

"You know... the stiff. The corpse. The dead body. The fuckin' cadaver they found in the storage unit above Broad Street Market the other day?" he said.

"No."

He nodded.

"The guy that owns the store had been rentin' out the storage space in the attic to some guy. I guess once the guy's wife kicked him out, he just started living up there. Him and his dog. It was just this tiny attic, you know. No floorboards in some areas. Just pink fiberglass insulation and shit."

Nick paused the game to light a cigarette.

"So one day he's sittin' up there, and his heart pops. Massive heart attack. He's dead before he can even take three paces to get out of his little cell. He never told nobody he was livin' up there, though. Nobody found the goddamn body until maggots starting rainin' down from the ceiling into the store a few weeks later."

Nick hissed a laugh between his teeth.

"Can't you just imagine some old lady perusing the fat-free dairy section when maggots start fallin' from the goddamn sky?"

"So what, his body like rotted through the floor or something?" I said.

Nick squinted.

"I ain't sure," he said. "Musta been something like 'at."

He tapped his cigarette on the rim of the ashtray and twirled it in his fingertips.

"You know what the worst part was, though?" he said.

"What?"

"The dog. The dog was trapped up there. Padlocked into

this tiny room. No windows or nothin'. No way out."

He shook his head.

"The dog ate part of the body, but... Must've whined and yowled like crazy, but I guess nobody could hear it. It starved eventually."

We were both quiet for a long time.

CHAPTER 2

I TOTALLY GET THE WHOLE bully thing. For the dumb people — the lowest common denominator — the whole world is made up of aggressors and their victims. You can only be one or the other, so you better be on the attack. They spend their days probing their peers for weakness. The aggressors find a wimp that won't stand up, and they proceed to push them around so they can feel some sense of power in the world. Control. It's a struggle for control that's so small. So meaningless...

Troy Summers is like the King of the lowest common denominator clan. Just look at his goddamn name! He sounds like he was born to play quarterback and be a total dick, right? Exactly. Well, he is at the top of the food chain, so he doesn't usually get hands-on with the actual losers. He gets to torment the other bullies, see, whom in turn have to take their aggression out on the rest of us.

Does anyone get any real satisfaction out of spitting in a kid's mashed potatoes and making him eat them, though? Is there real power or control in calling a fat kid "bitch titties" in the locker room? Or pissing in some kid's shoes while he is off in his gym clothes? Or writing "fag" with a sharpie on someone's locker?

Of course not. I have no control. You have no control. Troy Summers has no control. It's all bullshit, so who cares?

But then I stop myself. I think maybe this is just what I

think because I am a victim. Not that I'm the victim of something or someone in particular. I mean being a victim, like the archetype. Like I was somehow born to play this victim — predestined to be susceptible and weak — and it will shape how I see myself and how others see me forever. Almost like the runt of the litter, you know? I have a mark on me. It's invisible, but everyone can still see it somehow, like, subconsciously or something. Or maybe it's a smell. Like pheromones or whatever. A stench.

I am the one that always flinches.

See, I never take action, so I only have words. I can use them to convince myself that this whole struggle for control means nothing, but why do I never act? Why do I always freeze up? Does the world really work the way they think it does, and I'm already stuck on the losing end of the deal?

Is my destiny already etched in stone? Is it coded into my DNA? Like, biologically, I'm just a complete pussy and always will be?

I have to piss.

Back.

So what I was getting to was this: Today I was Troy Summers' victim. Yes, the King stooped low to rough up one of the mere peasants for once.

Don't get excited. It was nothing too elaborate.

We passed in the hall, and when I least expected it, he pushed me into the lockers. Yeah. Troy Summers is known for two things: upper body strength and the element of surprise. Anyway, I crashed into the cold metal so goddamn loud, my books flying everywhere.

See, I'm kind of big for my age — like 6'2", 190 or so — and sometimes the bullies, the jocks like Troy, in particular, don't like the idea that I'm bigger than them, so they lash out. They have a lot of pent up hostility from being cursed with being handsome, super popular and getting all the girls, I guess.

It was weird, though. For that first split second, I thought about attacking him. It flashed in my head — a quick lightning bolt of violent intent. But I looked up, and Troy glared back with that hawk look in his eye — maybe not quite as mean and dead-on-the-inside looking as Nick, but something like that. So I just went about gathering up my books, and he moved on. He didn't say anything, but his friends all laughed.

Good times.

◆　◆　◆

I can't stop thinking about Troy and getting pushed over and all of that. Actually, I should say that I can't stop thinking about that moment afterward. The moment of aggression welling up inside of me.

I don't know. I've never really felt anything quite like that before. It was like this crazy call to action. I mean, I didn't answer the call or whatever, but I think what scares me more is that looking back I think maybe I should have. There was violence in my heart, and I kind of wanted it there.

Yeah, yeah. I know everyone is a tough guy after the fact within the safety of their bedroom with a damn pen in their hand, but I don't know... I probably should just keep my head down like always and not think these things, right?

Right.

Casting Shadows Everywhere

◆　◆　◆

I was sitting in biology when I had my epiphany.

Mrs. Francis droned on and on about how mitochondria are the powerhouses of the cell. To call her a bore would somehow fail to capture the spirit of what she does with her lectures. Violently boring. She attacks us with it. Swings it with the intent to bludgeon. Biology taught via blunt force trauma.

Anyway, I guess I zoned out somewhere in there, let my thoughts drift out into the emptiness.

Or maybe not. Maybe I stopped thinking at all. Staunched this flow of words that endlessly leaks into my head.

Yes. Maybe it's only when you stop thinking, when you reach some place of total stillness, that you can even experience something like this.

When the epiphany hit, it made me suck in a breath, pulled all of my skin taut and sent strange tingles over my shoulders and down my spine.

It wasn't an idea so much as an instinct, something emotional, something primal. I just knew these things as though they were beamed into my head. Felt them more than thought them.

I want to change.

I want to transform.

Need to evolve, to morph, to start a revolution in my head.

I need to become something new. Need to.

I didn't think these words so much as simply know all of these things on some spiritual or religious level, feel them somewhere deep in my body, maybe deeper than my body. All the way down to the core of my being, of whatever I am.

I have to change now. Change myself. I don't know how

yet, but I know it's true. I've never been more sure of anything in my life.

And suddenly this euphoria came over me. I felt outside myself, outside of this classroom, outside of this group of students learning about the basics of biology.

I could observe them all as an outsider. All those impassive faces. Blank. Here but not really here, not really in the moment.

I could see the mundane reality of all of this written on those faces. See how this moment was something small. Something meaningless. Something all of us would forget soon.

And still, I felt light and giddy. Exhilarated and alive. The only brain stirring in this place, maybe. The only one awake.

I started laughing then. First it came out as silent little puffs, but soon it built to something I can only call an "insane giggle." I don't know why it was funny, but it was.

And all of those heads turned to look at me, puzzled faces occupying the place where the blankness had been.

I put my own head down, buried it in my arms, that shadow closing in around me. But I couldn't stop laughing.

◆　◆　◆

I tried to tell Nick about the bullies. About Troy and all the rest, and how I couldn't figure out what it meant about me. But I don't think I did a very good job explaining it.

He didn't say anything for a long time. In fairness, he was immersed in a Playstation shootout.

Blue smoke pirouetted off the end of his cigarette and slowly drifted up into the drop ceiling. Like all light colored items in the apartment, the textured white tiles of fire retardant

14

mineral fiber overhead were slowly but surely being stained nicotine yellow.

He paused the game to shove a handful of off-brand Honey BBQ Fritos into his mouth.

"Did you think about doin' anything?"

His words broke me out of a trance. I looked away from the ceiling.

"What?"

"When the guy knocked you down. I know you didn't do nothin', but did you think about it? Or were you just scared?"

I sipped at my Mountain Dew and thought about it.

"I did think about going for him... for a split second. But Troy is... I mean, nobody messes with Troy, you know?"

Nick turned back to the TV and unpaused the game.

"I'd be pissin' in his mouth after I knocked him out."

Nick says a lot of stuff like that. Like his whole life is an action movie. I didn't know what to say, but he went on.

"Look, it don't matter. Not really. It don't actually mean nothin' about you."

He said all this through a mouthful of barbecue flavored corn chips.

"Yeah?"

"Well, what he done to you is a fact. It is what it is. But what it means is just an idea. You can't change a fact, but you can always change an idea."

Not sure if that's really advice. He looked far away, and when he spoke again it was a mutter. I didn't feel like he was talking to me anymore.

"None of it means nothin', really."

We just sat for a while. He shot a guy in the face with a

machine gun. In the video game, I mean. Then he lit another cigarette.

♦ ♦ ♦

The ladies love Nick. Have I not mentioned that before? I guess I don't really get it. I mean, he has a big square chin like a damn cowboy, so I can see like a handsomeness or whatever there, but he also has gapped yellow teeth, bad skin and perpetually greasy dark hair hanging down in his eyes. He has a big shiny forehead. We're talking bulbous, dude. He can be pretty mean, too. Jesus, I know he's my cousin, but he's kind of a dirtbag.

I think he must have some of that "animal magnetism" they talk about on TV or something, though. 'Cause these girls... they're all over him, man. I definitely don't have that. Animal magnetism, I mean.

His current girlfriend is Tammie, who always seems to have a medicated feel about her. A slow warmth. She's too skinny, bleaches her hair, wears a shit ton of eyeliner and has bad teeth, but she is nice. I'm guessing she's a stripper, though I never really thought about that before and have no direct knowledge of such activities. I guess she just seems like the kind of person who would take off her clothes for money on a regular basis.

♦ ♦ ♦

Nick found me after school. Kinda weird. He was waiting about a half of a block down the street, smoking a cig.

"You wanna walk with me to the gas station?" he said.

"Sure."

The sky spat sprinkles of rain. We walked through the grass along the side of the road 'cause there were no sidewalks this way, and I slipped a couple times on the wet grass but managed to catch myself. No falls. No problems.

Nick slapped his hand along a row of mailboxes outside of a trailer park for senior citizens. It sounded like someone clapping, but you could hear the wet to it.

"I been thinkin' about what you were sayin'," he said. "About that kid knockin' you over."

"Yeah?"

He nodded.

"I think I can help you," he said. "Teach you."

"What, like fighting lessons?"

"Not exactly."

He wouldn't really go into detail, but my first lesson is supposed to be on Friday.

Weird how that works, huh? I put that want out into the universe — wanting to change — and look what happens?

♦ ♦ ♦

I am friends with this kid, Robert. Well, I mean, we're friends in gym class. Not friends outside of school type friends, you know? Yeah. Well, he's mildly autistic. Anyway, gym is the one class a day he has outside of Special Ed.

Today we were partners on one basketball hoop doing this George Mikan drill, which is gym teacher jargon for "shooting layups." Robert was talking about rappers that he likes.

"I like Lil' Wayne and Drake and Tupac Shakur," he said, pronouncing it correctly. "And Two Pack."

He really stressed the pronunciation of pack this time as in a pack of cigarettes.

I dribbled and shot the ball. It banked off the backboard, teetered on the rim and fell through the net. I passed the ball to Robert.

"Pretty sure those are the same guy," I said. "And they're both pronounced the same."

He shook his head. He always sports thick stubble and wears these goggles in gym. He's actually pretty intelligent on the whole, but he maintains a childlike understanding of the universe that somehow captures my imagination.

"One is spelled T-U-P-A-C and the other is the number 2-P-A-C. They're different. 2-pack-alypse now."

"He just changed the spelling, Robert. Like for artistic reasons."

He wrinkled his nose up and thought about it, squeezing the ball a second before he went back to firing up layups.

"No. I think they're different. Tupac Shakur and Two Pack."

"Maybe you're right," I said. I didn't even want to get into the whole Makaveli thing.

He is so much more curious about the world around him than the other kids I know. And, like, enthusiastic. He exudes none of the ironic detachment or whatever you want to call it that all these jerkoffs do. He is not "too cool" to connect with the world. He attempts to do so in earnest. Constantly.

I tried a more elaborate underhand scoop style layup and missed.

"What church do you go to?" Robert said.

He is a fan of abrupt changes in the topic of conversation.

"I don't go to church."

He recoiled, letting the ball bounce away from us. He jogged after it and squinted at me on the way back. One of those accusatory squints people usually save for someone who stole something from them.

"Jake. Are you a Christian?"

The truth is that I'm not. I'm not one of those militantly ball-busting atheist kids or anything. It's not even something I give much thought, really. I figure I'm never going to know, so what's the point in thinking about it?

I sensed that I couldn't tell Robert this, though.

"Well, yeah," I said. "Not all Christians go to church, you know? What really matters is your relationship with God."

Robert looked up at the gym ceiling hanging above us, and then made eye contact with me for a second before nodding his approval.

CHAPTER 3

FIRST LESSON TODAY. PRETTY INTENSE. I went to Nick's after school. Donnie was getting ready for work, and by "getting ready for work" I mean he was rolling a bunch of cigarettes.

He perched on the edge of one of the recliners with a bag of tobacco balanced on one knee and a bag of empty cigarette tubes on the other.

Donnie packed a wad of tobacco in one side of this little gray and blue plastic thing and pushed this lever on top, and the machine jammed a load of tobacco into each tube. I use the term "machine" somewhat loosely as this baby was powered solely by elbow grease.

He looked up and noticed me watching.

"They kinda taste like ass, but it works out to like one-third of the price of Camels," he said.

After Donnie took off, I pestered Nick about my first lesson.

"So what's the plan?" I asked.

He didn't respond.

He was reading this book about the Hare Krishnas. He only reads non-fiction. Also, he's like insanely good at ignoring me when he wants to. So I just sat there.

There's this big crack in the painted over wallpaper running down one of their walls, with like a tributary of smaller cracks branching off of it. It's white paint over this green and gold wallpaper, which you can see bits of through the crack. I think it must be water damage related 'cause there are all of these little bubbled up spots along it. Anyway, Nick took his sweet time reading so I got a real good look at that wall. Rest assured that it was much more boring than what I have captured here.

Eventually he put the damn book down and stood up. He did this stretching move with his back and it made a series of disgusting sounding cracks.

He walked to the door and opened it and then stared at me, like I was just supposed to know we were leaving.

I sprang off the couch and followed him out the door.

"So where are we going, then?" I said. I was excited but kind of nervous, too.

"You'll see."

That's all he would say.

We climbed into his car, a purple Chevy Malibu. Or maybe really dark blue, I guess. We rolled down through town, and...

You know what? I'm going to go ahead and just definitively state that the car is, in fact, dark blue. Can't really picture Nick with a purple car now that I think about it.

Anyway, we rolled through town, and I was kind of expecting that we'd maybe stop at a park or something. See, I was still totally hung up on the fight training idea. I mean, I kind of knew it wouldn't be that, but I guess I couldn't think of what else it would be.

I think somewhere in my imagination I had a montage rolling where I'd drink a couple of raw eggs, run up a bunch of steps, work the heavy bag a bit, and I'd be ready to knock some damn teeth out.

We just kept going, though. All the way through town on

Carelton and out toward the country. And the only thing out that way is Wal-Mart.

Shit. My mom is calling me. Hang on.

◆ ◆ ◆

Hm... So I took out the garbage last night and ended up watching TV.

So yeah... let me finish this first lesson story.

We pulled into the back of the Wal-Mart parking lot. I got the feeling that Nick wanted to park far enough back to be out of everyone's way, but not so far as to potentially arouse suspicion. He got all quiet again.

We just sat in the Malibu. Across the aisle, a college girl in green sweatpants packed her groceries into the back of her Volvo and drove away.

After that, I undid my seat belt and swung my shoulders to face toward the front door of the building.

The people by the door looked small from this far away. Lines of them marched in and out of the store like ants, pushing carts and carrying shopping bags to and from the sprawling rows of cars.

Minivans and station wagons drove in and out at a rhythmic pace, like the parking lot was inhaling and exhaling soccer moms.

"Promise me you'll do what I tell you today," Nick said.

I swung back around to face him.

"What?"

"Look, I just mean... After this you can quit if you want. I'd understand. I'd have no problem with that. But today... If you want my help, you gotta go through with this, all right?"

"Uh... yeah, I guess."

"Say 'Nick, I want your help, and I promise I'll do what you say,' then."

"What the hell? What's with all this promising stuff? You're freaking me out."

"I know that you won't want to do it, so I want you to promise ahead of time."

"But doesn't telling me that kind of defeat the whole purpose of... Oh, whatever. Nick, I promise to do whatever you say."

He rubbed at the stubble on his chin and smiled.

"Good. Now go in there and steal somethin'."

"But..."

The Earth opened up. Stars collided. Cities burned. There were rolling blackouts up and down the Eastern seaboard.

But in the Malibu? Only silence.

So maybe my Mom was right about the whole bad influence thing after all.

"I told you that you wouldn't want to do it. But you promised. Look, I know it don't make much sense at the moment. Think of this like a football coach pushin' his players 'til they want to puke. They hate him. He's askin' too much, and they don't want to do it. But ain't that the whole point? They push themselves harder and farther than they believed possible. They come out of it lean and hard, and I'm talkin' mentally as much as physically, and they ultimately respect the coach like a father figure for gettin' the most out of them."

"I didn't realize that you were Mike Ditka now. Wait. Don't you hate sports?"

"This is what I'm sayin': Doin' stuff you's scared to do and succeeding builds confidence like nothin' else."

"OK, Dr. Phil. What about doing things you're scared to do and getting arrested for shoplifting?"

Nick reached around his seat and dug out a warm can of Monster from somewhere on the floor. He cracked the can open. He is the only adult I know who drinks energy drinks. The car filled with that artificial, almost bubble-gummy Monster smell. He took a big slurp and shrugged.

"Don't get caught."

"Great advice. So what should I steal?"

"Don't matter."

"Right. Yeah... OK."

"Don't over think it. Just walk in there, snatch something, shove that shit in your pocket and walk out. Fortune favors the motherfuckin' bold, Jake. The more brazen you is about doin' it, the better."

I stepped out of the Malibu and stretched to stall for a few seconds before I closed the door. Arching my back, I stared into the gray clouds of dusk above. One of the massive parking lot lights glowed down on me, and the bravest of the local insects swarmed around the lamp like a hundred little Icarus copy-cats trying their best to fly into the sun.

Finally striding toward the store, I started to get all of those little nervous feelings: sweaty palms, churning butterfly stomach and the bloat of what felt like explosive diarrhea swelling just below that. Panic rolled over me in waves.

But when I looked around, no one in the lot was paying any attention to me, even with my eyes probably shifting around like crazy. No one cared.

I reached up to brush at my eyebrow, and the coldness of my fingers startled me. Adrenaline. I remember learning on an episode of Law & Order or some other cop show that when you get a rush of adrenaline, the temperature in your hands can drop 10 or 15 degrees in a matter of seconds. It's apparently a good way to tell if someone is lying.

The door slid open in front of me, and as I crossed the threshold a little old man with an oxygen tank said, "Good evening, folks." I guess he thought I was with the Hispanic family entering in front of me. I didn't make eye contact with the greeter, even though I thought that might seem more suspicious.

Have I not mentioned that I'm a huge pussy? 'Cause yeah. I could hear my heartbeat in my ears slamming as fast as the super clicky kick drum in a Cradle of Filth song. I guess it goes without saying that I've never stolen anything.

The first actual product I laid eyes on? DVDs. A big display of cheap DVDs just inside the door with a variety of Steve Martin movies and buns and Tae Bo related exercise videos. I knew I couldn't steal one of those, though. DVD cases have that magnetic strip that sets off the alarm by the door. Plus my buns are already in top condition, so it would be unnecessary. (OK, not really.)

Anyway... I never actually shop at Wal-Mart 'cause they are terrible human beings, so I wasn't really familiar with the layout.

I wandered through the women's clothing section and wound up near pet stuff. Thought about snagging a collar or something, but we don't have any pets 'cause we're not allowed to have them in our apartment building, so that seemed pretty

25

pointless.

Walked through the garden stuff. It's pretty much impossible, obviously, to conceal a plant on your person, but I did consider, however briefly, trying to shove a Chia Head in my pants. I pictured Nick saying, "Is that a Chia Head in your pants or are you just happy to see me?" which seemed extra funny 'cause he doesn't joke around very often. I couldn't help but start laughing.

So at that point I was aimlessly shuffling around Wal-Mart, giggling to myself like a crazy person and desperately looking for something — anything — to steal. This is what my life has become.

I speed-walked through the sporting goods section, and just as I got to the end of the aisle with baseball mitts, an enormous blue smocked figure stepped forth to block my path.

A red-headed giant with a scraggly orange beard like a Viking stood before me. He did a double take, his eyes met mine, and his giant mouth moved to speak. I totally expected him to slam a hockey stick down and scream in my face:

"You! Shall not! Pass!"

But he actually said:

"Y'all need help finding anything?"

His voice was higher than I expected, but I still almost spontaneously died of fright.

"I'm good," I said.

My voice sounded shaky, so I cleared my throat like I had a cold causing my weakened speech and not a vagina.

Something about the encounter made the whole thing real again, though. Snapped me out of the shock of this crazy situation. And I knew right then I couldn't steal anything. I mean, I never do these kinds of things. I can't. I never have, and I probably never will. Have the stones or whatever.

I thought about elementary school when Chad Hooper pushed me into the chain link fence over and over, and tears formed in my eyes and my breath heaved through my teeth and my hands squeezed into hard little fists at my sides. And I felt my body going through all the motions of an aggressive response, but I couldn't do it. I felt disconnected from it. My body wracked into place like a loaded shotgun aimed at his maggoty face, but I couldn't pull the trigger. And he laughed at me. At my eyes and my breathing and my fists. Laughed in my face and pushed me again.

The memory sparked something in my imagination, though. It felt like that flash of bad intentions after Troy pushed me down. And for that moment I didn't care anymore. Maybe when you hate yourself this much, you never have anything to lose.

I turned a corner near the office crap, and there they were. A pack of Gelly Roll Stardust Bold Galaxy pens. To be honest, I didn't realize the pens were of the Stardust Bold Galaxy variety at the time, nor was I previously familiar with the Gelly Roll brand of pen. I didn't get a good look at them, and I guess I wasn't thinking about much. I remember thinking "Pens!" and I just shoved the pens into my thankfully large back pocket and turned to leave.

I moved toward the door. I was trying to look bold, since I'm told fortune favors ballsiness above all else, but I'm pretty sure my eyes were twitching in a way that could only be considered "less than bold." It was like I couldn't stop blinking or something. I don't know.

I tried to walk slow, 'cause I felt like moseying along looked way less sketchy than hightailing it out of there, but my pace kept speeding up, probably trying to match my heartbeat which was now nearing mach speed.

The final ninety feet took a lifetime. The greeter swiveled his back to me as he turned to help an old lady separate a couple of tangled shopping carts. I accelerated like a running back hitting a seam off tackle and practically ran to daylight. Just as the door slid open, the greeter turned and half-yelled in a gruff voice, "Thank you!"

My heart shat itself.

But I was free.

I won't lie. Walking back through that parking lot was total euphoria. When I got back in the Malibu, Nick smirked at me.

"You've got the glow of a first-time thief, but where's your haul?"

I pulled out the pens and dropped them in his lap. His smirk faded.

"Gelly pens?"

He picked up the package and turned it over in his hands.

"Stardust Bold Galaxy?"

I realized for the first time that the pens were all colors like sea foam green and aqua. Not a single black in the pack.

"Why'd you steal these?"

"These are, uh, quality pens."

I looked at the price tag.

"They're like $10, so..."

"These are incredibly gay pens, Jake. Are you gay?"

"No."

"Are you sure? 'Cause it ain't like people get to choose that or whatever. I wouldn't have a problem with it or anything like that."

"I'm not gay. I just grabbed some pens without really looking."

"All right."

He tossed the pens back to me and started the car.

"So why do you think I had you do this?"

"I don't know. Maybe 'cause it's a rush."

We curved out of the lot and into traffic.

"Kind of, but it's more than that. It's like a lot of shit you've been told in your life is a lie. All these rules and all these things you worry about... they ain't got real meanin' on their own. The only meanin' they got is what we give 'em, you know?"

I nodded, but I only kind of got it. A homeless guy on the side of the road wiggled an orange sign at us to try to get us to buy crappy pizza from Little Caesar's.

"So you stole these gay pens from Wal-Mart, and you got away with it. In a way it's like it didn't even happen, you know? There ain't no spiritual or supernatural punishment comin' for you. It's over, and all that's left to show are the pens. As far as Wal-Mart knows, it never happened, and it ain't exactly like you're going to be decimated with guilt over stealin' from the richest company in the goddamn world, either, which I guess is maybe beside the point, but... Do you see what I'm gettin' at?"

"I think so."

"There ain't no magic power that makes right and wrong have real meanin' is all. I mean police and prisons keep order to a degree in a real world way, but on the most basic level, there's no order in this world like they try to say there is. None. It's chaos. Now I coulda told you that repeatedly, but I don't think it really strikes you until you go out and feel it for yourself. You crossed a line today. A boundary or whatever you want to call it. And now you can feel the truth of it in your gut — none of the rules are real. None of 'em."

We were silent for a moment, the sky blackening around us like burnt chicken skin.

"I want you to take a week and think about this. And if you want to learn more, I can teach more. If not? That's cool, too."

For the record, I still haven't decided.

CHAPTER 4

I CAN'T BELIEVE I HAVEN'T mentioned her in this journal yet: Beth Horne.

Yeah.

Like an idiot I fell for the first blonde-haired, blue-eyed girl who paid attention to me. We're just friends, of course. To her, anyway. We sit together in art class and history. She is a total achiever. I mean, I get good grades, but she's popular and everything. A homecoming queen-to-be. The perfect goddamn all-American girl that I have no chance with. So of course I'm in love.

Balls.

I don't mean to give the wrong impression, though. She's not an airhead like the other popular girls. She's smart. And she laughs really hard at funny things, which I think is kinda rare for a girl, you know? It seems like a lot of girls don't let themselves laugh very hard, in my school at least.

She even says funny stuff. Like today at lunch (she sits with me sometimes) we had the following conversation:

Beth: "Cats have no butt cheeks."

Me: "I can confirm the accuracy of that statement."

Beth: "No, I mean, they have nothing there. When a cat sits down, it is putting its actual asshole on the floor."

I laughed.

Me: "So you've got this little friend walking around, smearing his anus on your stuff."

Beth: "Smearing!"

The word could barely make it out of her mouth. She laughed so hard I thought Dr. Pepper might come out of her nose.

It didn't.

Oh. Also her boobs are huge, if I didn't already mention that. So that's pretty cool, too.

◆　◆　◆

Thinking about Nick's animal magnetism or whatever again.

At least Beth doesn't like him. She always says he's a creep whenever I bring him up.

Not that the guys that she likes are any better, I guess. Like today in art class we were talking about how insane it is that some guys wear skinny jeans. We were complaining together about bulges and what not, you know, and everything was going just fine. Then she started talking about how she likes guys that have kind of the skater look — hoodies and kinda baggie jeans or whatever. That's pretty much how I dress, so I was all like, "Hell yeah!"

But then she says:

"I mean say like Troy Summers... what he wears... I like his style."

Yeah.

The whole world crashed to a halt like in a movie trailer for a shitty comedy when there's the sound of the record needle scratching out of the groove and the music suddenly stops. Exactly like that.

My instinct was to get all quiet, but I didn't want her to

know that I was upset or whatever, so I had to kind of try to act normal. I had to stay in G-mode. She could tell something was a little off I think, but I don't think she put it all together. So that's good.

How lame is it that the preppiest douche kids totally stole what used to be an "alternative" style, though? All the preppie clothes look a lot like skater clothes. Now the only alternative is skin tight pants that make it look like you're smuggling plums. Unbelievable. Not that I really give a shit about clothes, but whatever.

◆　　◆　　◆

Today in English, we talked about turning points. Like in fiction, I mean.

The story sort of sets you up to expect one thing and then clobbers you with a big ol' turning point. Moments of change. They happen in a flash, rearrange how you perceive everything that came before, and the real deal turning points change the story in a way that cannot be altered. They're permanent. Like a chemical reaction, you know? You pour your vinegar into some baking soda, and it froths all over. You can't separate the elements anymore. Once it's done, it can't be undone.

The teacher, Mr. Chalmers, said every scene turns, at least in something well-written. I never thought of it that way before, but it makes sense. A scene starts in one place and ends in another — sometimes literally, sometimes tonally, sometimes it's a shift in emotions or values. The author mixes up the chemicals of character and plot, though, and it sets up a chain of reactions, both large and small. Displacement.

Combustion. Fire. Explosions.

And then in the bigger sense, the story itself turns. Like in a TV show, this is super easy to see — there's usually a cliffhanger just before the commercial break, right? Those are the act breaks and generally the places when the story turns, more often than not. Those are bigger than the scene turning points, too. We're talking about the seismic shifts, I guess. Those moments when the fault lines open up and the very ground under the character's feet becomes malleable. *Everything* changes. "Luke, I'm your father," and shit like that.

The point, above all, is for the reader to get a dramatic sense of movement.

According to Mr. Chalmers, all art boils down to implied movement. The best literature. The best paintings. The best music. It gives a sense of movement, of change we see and hear and feel. Something visceral. Something clear.

I think I used to think of these moments as "twists," but turning point is a better term. More specific.

'Cause everything hinges on that one little point, doesn't it? What came before and what came after, they change in a single second.

Usually the stuff the teachers say in school flees my mind the second the bell rings. I quickly clear that space for video games and such. But this stuck with me all day. I keep tumbling the idea in my head. Turning points.

The more I think about it, the more it seems plain that real life is filled to the brim with turning points. Like sticking those pens in my pocket. I reached my turning point right then and there.

I made my choice. I changed my story.

So what happens next?

Well, now I've got another turning point looming on the horizon. To learn these lessons from Nick or not. I don't know.

Part of me wants it. I know that much. Another part of me is maybe scared, though. Do I really want to be like Nick? I'm not sure.

And is this one of this little turning points? Or will the Earth open up beneath my feet if I make the wrong choice?

◆   ◆   ◆

I've been meaning to make a list of the things I like about Beth. It seems important to remember these things, you know? To record them so you can never forget. Even if things change.

- I like how she doesn't wear makeup ever when most girls in school cake their goddamn faces with it like they're about to go on live television.
- I like how when she's excited she talks all fast and even stutters sometimes.
- I like how she whispers to herself when she thinks no one can hear.
- I like that she likes horror movies even though they scare the crap out of her.
- I like how she laughs until she cries sometimes. Literally. Streaming tears and beet red face and everything.
- I like how she smiles at me when she knows I'm nervous to try to make me feel better.
- I like how she describes things. Like if we both saw a

house, later I'd say it was a brick house, but she would have taken a picture with her mind and described every detail: the chipped paint on the banister, the way the floor of the porch sagged in the middle, the types of flowers and ivy growing along it, the tree branches reaching out over the roof, the way the shadows leaned on the bricks and shutters, the sound of the wind chimes and the smell of the smoke billowing out from under the lid of the grill.

- I like how when she smiles, there is a dimple on one cheek but not the other.
- I like how she laughs at things that are actually funny and not at every dumb thing.
- I like how she doesn't get all bored or tune out when I start talking about video games, even though I know it's super boring to listen to someone talk about video games.
- I like that her fingers are super long like crazy spider hands.
- I like that she likes watching the same crappy reality TV shows as me.
- I like that she enjoys discussing said crappy reality shows at length with me.
- I like her nose.
- I like the way my world feels whole when she is around.
- I like knowing that she is out there in the universe when she is not around.

CHAPTER 5

I went back to Nick's today, but he wasn't there, so I just hung out with Tammie for a while. She is actually a lot smarter than I thought. We watched Dr. Oz talk about how to eliminate belly bloat, and she kept offering to get me something to eat or drink, but I wasn't hungry, you know. Eventually an old fashioned conversation broke out.

"You don't have a girlfriend, do you?" she said. She picked at the pilled up spots on her pajama pants.

"No. I like that you can just tell that about me, though. Makes a guy feel real good about himself."

She laughed.

"Nah. I can tell that you're the shy type, though, so I figured."

"The shy, girlfriend-less type. That's me."

"You just need to show some confidence. That's what wins girls over."

"Yeah."

"Girls want to believe they're getting with a guy who's going places. A lot of people think that there are a bunch of gold-digging girls out there, but I think girls want to feel like they're getting on board a ride, you know. Something exciting. Like your life together will be an adventure the two of you will go on. So it's more about confidence and success than money, at least most of the time."

"I guess that makes sense."

"It's kind of a flaw in some ways. Girls always end up getting drawn to the selfish guys instead of the nice guys, you know?"

"Right."

I thought about making a joke about Nick being the most selfish person ever, but she had a troubled look in her eye, so I let it go.

We played video games after that. She is actually pretty good. I mean, I beat her pretty mercilessly most of the time, but I've seen worse.

◆ ◆ ◆

Tammie turned the stove on and set the frying pan on the burner with a clatter.

"See, the problem with a lot of guys is they're too nice," she said.

She scooped a blob of margarine out of a yellow tub with a fork and plopped it into the pan. It sizzled as it hit the hot metal.

I frowned and scratched my eyebrow.

"So... I should be a dick?"

Tammie laughed. She always closed her eyes and scrunched up her shoulders when she laughed. It reminded me of the way a little kid would laugh.

"No, I don't mean that. Being nice is okay, but there's *too* nice."

She cracked three eggs into the pan in rapid succession and started stirring them with the fork.

"It's like... when you like someone, you want to know

everything about them, right?"

I nodded.

"Well, the Too Nice Guys, I think they've already got this idea in their head of the girls they like. It's like, their girl is perfect. But nobody's perfect. So it makes you feel like... like they don't know you at all, and they never could. They just like this imaginary perfect girl in their head, you know? And if they did figure out what you were really like, then maybe they wouldn't like it so much. So even though someone thinking you're perfect may sound good, it's not."

She pushed the gooey egg clumps around in the pan with the fork. I almost told her she shouldn't use the fork like that because it wrecks the non-stick coating on the pan (at least this is what my mom always shrieks at me), but I stopped myself.

"Everybody wants to feel special and loved. But you sort of need to feel like you've earned it."

◆　◆　◆

My parents got divorced when I was five. I visited my dad every two weeks for a couple years. That deteriorated to every six or eight weeks for a while, and I haven't seen him at all since I was ten. I guess that's how Nick became the guy I looked up to most so early on. Like my role model or whatever. I mean, Nick was there.

But I know enough now to know that Nick is not the ideal role model at all. It's like he has this missing piece that makes him not all the way human. And that is what makes him so impervious to pain, you know? Like no one can hurt him, but I think it also means that he can never really connect to other people, not in the way that normal people do. He can't let his guard down and let someone else see the vulnerable pieces underneath, because there is only guard and nothing else. The vulnerable pieces don't exist for him.

Like I already said, Nick gets with lots of girls, but when I think about the idea of Nick being in love with one of them, it makes me laugh. It's just not possible. That piece of him is gone, gone, gone.

Sometimes I think the closest Nick gets to connecting with another person is with me. I mean, he wants to help me, you know. Wants to protect me and teach me to protect myself. I've never seen him do anything like that before. Anything remotely nurturing. I think I am the only one that he can see himself in a little bit. The only person he can identify with in a way.

So I started to think that maybe we could wind up helping each other. Like he could toughen me up, but I could teach him something, too.

Christ. What have I been thinking? If I journey into Nick's world, maybe I can never come back. I can never undo how it changes me. And what happens if I come out of there with missing pieces of my own?

So the debate rages on.

I was thinking about Nick as my sort of male role model and how fucked up that would be. But then I kind of reviewed the other options in my mind:

My Dad — Don't really know this guy. Obviously he's not super loyal. Additionally, he kind of seemed like a pussy from what I remember. He possesses neither the can-do spirit nor the stick-to-it-iveness that I look for in the rugged individual I wish to look up to.

Uncle Ray — My uncle Ray works construction. He is 43 and has never been in a serious relationship. His house is full of vintage pornography of all kinds that he desperately tries to conceal whenever my mom and I stop by his place. His primary hobby is making intricate birdhouses and selling them at flea markets and booths at county fairs. His secondary hobby is getting black-out drunk every night.

Terry — Terry is one of those unofficial uncles who is really just a family friend. He has been divorced twice. He wears cargo shorts and denim shirts all the time as though he is going on a safari instead of going to Wal-Mart. He does not strike me as a reader. One time he said "infimite wisdom" instead of infinite wisdom. He got shards of glass in his eyes somehow a long time ago, so he is on disability and hasn't had a real job since about 1997.

In comparison, Nick doesn't seem so bad. He does whatever he wants to do all the time.

◆　◆　◆

Somehow I slept through my alarm this morning. Usually I mix up a huge coffee with tons of milk and sugar in it. Like Big Gulp sized in one of those travel coffee mugs that is basically a stainless steel pitcher. But I didn't have time for that, so I was late to school and still half asleep.

Luckily I'm at JCC on Tuesday mornings. I trod in a good fifteen minutes late, and the professor didn't even look at me.

"So the conditioned reflex, in this case, is that the dogs salivate when Pavlov rings the bell," he said.

I guess I didn't fully explain this before — I'm taking this college class, Psychology 100, at Jefferson Community College on Tuesdays and Thursdays. Really, sophomores aren't supposed to be allowed to dual enroll and take college classes for high school credit. Only honor roll seniors.

But I realized that one of the guidance counselors, Mr. Pinkett, essentially doesn't give a shit anymore. If you fill out the paperwork, he will sign it. No questions asked. (That's also how I got into Beth's art class.) Mr. Pinkett mentioned that his wife "walked out on" him "out of the blue after twenty years of beautiful marriage" a couple of times, so I assume that pushed him over the edge and into this radical state of apathy and possibly even drinking on the job (total speculation, but he always has this big thermos with him).

"You're now more likely to hear this referred to as classical conditioning," the professor said.

He pinched a tiny piece of chalk in his fingers and scrawled the words on the blackboard in sloppy cursive letters.

"Pavlov's experiment became the backbone of behaviorism, which was the dominant school of thought in psychology until the cognitive revolution later on in the 20th century, but I suppose that's for later in the semester. I'll try not to get ahead of myself."

Classes at the community college are way laid back compared to the confrontational air of high school classrooms. Anything goes.

For example, there's this short pale guy who sits in front of me. He's probably at least 35 years old judging by the salt and pepper stubble. He always sports the same beanie, Detroit Pistons shorts and Adidas sandals and eats a bag of either Munchos or Funyuns every class. (I'd say it's Funyuns two out of three times so far.)

Anyway, it's rad. It makes all the stuff in high school about no hats and no food or drinks seem like utter bullshit.

Sir Funyuns raised his hand.

"How come Pavlov loved messin' with these dogs so much?"

He stuck a Funyun in his mouth before he was even done asking the question.

The professor just chuckled.

He's pretty interesting, too. Mr. Sanderson.

"You bring up an interesting point. Something that all scientists have to consider when they're conducting an experiment."

He pulled at his wispy white beard, turned his stooped shoulders to the blackboard and hesitated a moment before chalking out "ETHICS" in all caps.

He apparently used to do behavioral psychology lab experiments at various universities around the country. He made sure to overtly imply that, while at one such research engagement, he banged the lady who wrote our textbook. That's kind of funny, but I imagine the same quality of character that led him to brag to a bunch of college (and high school) kids about sex stuff landed him at a community college, while she pens textbooks for major publishers.

"One of my colleagues when I was doing research at the University of Maryland made a major behavioral psych breakthrough, and earned himself considerable acclaim, in an experiment that involved flash freezing a rat's brain."

His forehead turned into a pile of wrinkles with two puffy white caterpillars of eyebrows climbing toward his hairline.

"A live rat's brain," he said, wiggling the chalk in the air for emphasis.

He paused a moment, letting the silence in the room creep toward something awkward for dramatic effect.

"That's certainly something PETA and the like would find unethical, yes?"

In any case, it turns out that psychology is awesome. It's by far my best class. Some of the theory part reads a little dry, but the science of the brain rocks.

Everything that we do wires pathways in our brains. So every time you practice a song on a guitar, you are wiring that into your brain, and each time you practice it, the wiring grows more intricate, more precise. That's why you improve over time. That's why repetition and practice lead to success in all things. Eventually the wiring perfects itself and your fingers just know where to go. You don't think about it anymore. It becomes a part of you.

I can't believe I've gone through my life not knowing this.

◆　　◆　　◆

Robert hit with me a real doozy today. The gym teacher had us doing laps around the basketball court to get warmed up before we played dodgeball. Robert and I stuck together toward the back of the pack like we usually do.

"Hey Jake, I've got a question," Robert said.

"Go for it."

"What's butt chugging?"

Wow. I had no goddamn idea how to respond.

"Where'd you hear that?" I said.

44

"On TV. The news. This kid got in trouble for butt chugging at college, and everyone is mad at him and stuff, but I don't even know what butt chugging is."

We were silent for a quarter of a lap with only the sounds of tennis shoes clattering on hardwood echoing all around us.

"Is it like..." he said before trailing off.

I couldn't fathom the idea of him trying to imagine what the words "butt chugging" might mean, so I interrupted his thoughts. Not that the reality is much better in this case, I guess.

"Well, you know how people — some people — drink alcohol, like beer and whiskey and stuff, to get drunk?"

He nodded.

"My Dad drinks Heineken," he said. "You know Heineken? In the green bottles? I tried it once, but... It tasted real bad. I like Vernors."

"Yeah. Vernors. That's good stuff," I said. "But yeah, some people figured out that you can kind of drink beer through your ass. That's butt chugging. It makes them get drunk really fast or something."

I paused a second to let that sink in.

"It's really dumb and dangerous, though, so I'm never going to do that, and you're never going to do that, right?" I said.

Robert didn't say anything for a long time. We finished our laps and stood in a line along the bleachers to await further gym instruction.

"But why do they do it?" he finally said.

"I don't know," I said. "They just want to get drunk really fast."

45

He picked at the strap on his goggles, so I could tell he was getting upset.

"Only like really dumb people do it," I said. "It's not cool. At all."

Robert slowly started shaking his head. His lips puckered into a frown like he'd tasted something sour.

He was definitely a little rattled, but I still think it made more sense to just tell him the truth. I really can't protect him from the world. No one can protect him all the time, you know? All this crazy shit exists out there, and he's going to pick up on these weird bits and pieces and try to figure out how they fit into the way he sees the universe. All I can do is try my best to help him understand.

◆　◆　◆

My dad sent me an email about eight months ago out of nowhere. After no contact for five years or however long. He talked about missing me, and how he's a bad father, and how he could understand if I don't want anything to do with him. He rattled off a bunch of happy memories about us, I guess he was getting pretty sentimental, but all of the events he mentioned happened before I was five. So they mean nothing to me, you know? I literally don't remember them... most of them, at least.

And I kind of realized that his pain is real or whatever, but his pain isn't over the loss of me as an individual. It's over the loss of the role of a son. He doesn't know me, so none of it connects to me. It's a loss in his imagination, you know? Like all of the ideals and hopes people project onto their children?

He lost all that. But that's not me.

I don't know. Maybe to someone else, these things sound weepy or bitter or angry. But I don't mean them that way.

Anyway, I didn't write back, but it got me thinking. At this point I have probably spent more time in my life watching McDonald's and Wal-Mart commercials than I've spent talking to my own father. Kinda weird, you know?

Like I am this super specific genetic material. My DNA is unique and could only come from my precise mom and dad. Out of the billions of years the Earth has existed and the billions of people on the planet currently, I am here now and I come directly from these two people. And even so I have spent more time being told to "watch out for falling prices" at Wal-Mart and heard "I'm loving it" from Ronald McDonald and his minions than I have conversing with this person who I came from.

I actually read about McDonald's advertising strategies in some book. Their goal is to seem like a "trusted friend." That kinda creeps me out.

After reading it, I immediately remembered this particular commercial where a young couple is eating at McDonald's, and the girlfriend asks some awkward question. The boyfriend hesitates. He's stumped. A voice-over voice chimes in to reassure the boyfriend by saying, "You got this." The boyfriend throws out an answer and takes a big bite of a burger. The girlfriend seems appeased. She eats a fry. The voice congratulates the boyfriend by saying, "Well played."

So I guess that disembodied voice is the voice of McDonald's comforting this guy. Because McDonald's is his trusted friend. And if we're watching the commercial, they must be our trusted friend, too.

And over the course of my life, they've concocted thousands of these scenarios to indirectly communicate this message to me over and over and over again. They beat that idea into my brain starting with the commercials for Happy Meals when I watched cartoons as a toddler. As I got older, they used more sophisticated ads to reach me regarding Big Macs and McNuggets when I watched shows geared for the 13-34 demographic.

They were always there for me. In good times and bad. Always looking for new ways to teach that fundamental message to me. To wire themselves into the fabric of my identity.

So I guess in a certain way, it's like McDonald's took the place of my dad.

Well played.

CHAPTER 6

I DREAMED OF ZOMBIES FRICKIN' everywhere last night. Pretty cliché, actually. The dead stalked the streets, wanting nothing more than to eat the hell out of some brains. I somehow knew that I had to sneak into the Horne home, grab a sleeping Beth by the hand and lead her away from a couple of zombie cops in hot brain pursuit.

We weaved through the mess of ravaged cars cluttering the streets. Horns blared from the corpses resting on various steering wheels. Blinkers blinked all around.

Zombies clambered over cars to close in on us, but they kept losing their footing and doing hilarious *Home Alone* style falls onto the pavement.

When we got downtown, the mall burned, and all the zombies around there were on fire and screaming. Endless screaming. And really pained and shrill. Not the usual zombie moan that can be a bit passionless. Thick black smoke everywhere.

The next thing I knew, the smoke cleared, and we were racing down stone steps into this castle basement with one of those huge metal doors like a walk-in fridge in a grocery store meat department. I turned a crank to seal the door and even fastened a padlock onto a latch for good measure.

Zombies banged at the door and moaned, but we were safe. And then Beth wrapped her arms around me, and she didn't say anything, but I knew that she loved me because I saved her and everything, and I felt all warm and tingly.

When I woke up, I was really disappointed that it wasn't real. Reality is the only true nightmare.

◆　◆　◆

I'm not really into all that sexy stuff. Don't get me wrong. I am a heterosexual adolescent male with a fully functional set of testicles pumping out testosterone and matching penis pumping out jizz. And sometimes when I see a hot girl I get so excited that my balls quiver on the brink of explosion. So it's not like I'm some kind of prude or what have you.

But say today in the hall, I was minding my own business. This farmer kid, Chris Redd, walked next to me. Out of nowhere, he visibly recoiled. Like a spasm traveled up his body and stopped him dead in his tracks. He gasped. I followed his gaze to the end of the hall where Renee McElwee bent over to pick up her books. Her skirt rode up and turquoise underwear peeked out of the bottom. Chris Redd turned to me and said:

"Jesus! Is that Renee McElwee?! God, dude. I would rip those panties off and pound that shit."

My initial reaction was, "Uh... Is this guy talking to me?" I looked around. No one else lurked nearby, so I guess he was. I didn't know what to say, so I just said:

"Yeah."

I don't know. I guess I don't get that level of aggression over sex stuff. I mean, first of all, this guy chose to share this information with a stranger. That's a weird lack of impulse control. Second, what's with the violent language, you know? Way more ripping and pounding going on than I'm comfortable with, to be frank.

When she finally gathered up her books, and she took her time in my opinion, he smiled and slapped me on the back like we'd just shared something together. Like we bonded over this girl's ass, and we'd forever exchange knowing glances over the time that Renee bent over in the hallway.

Dude. Gross. I don't know what goes on in farm country, but in my neighborhood we keep our creepy leering to ourselves and don't do group high fives every time there's cleavage in the vicinity. Sheesh.

◆　◆　◆

It's decided. I said I wanted to change, right? Well, here we go.

Friday I will go to Nick's apartment after school. I will put in a formal request for another lesson. (Doubt he has a syllabus or I would ask for that.) This could be the dumbest choice I've made in my fifteen years, but I don't know. I feel desperate maybe. Frustrated. It's time to act.

So I will dive headfirst into something new. I will sit on my hands no longer. I will reach out, grab the world by the shoulders, wrestle it to the goddamn ground, and I will do... something.

I will do something. I will do anything. 'Cause take it from me: Anything is better than nothing. Nothing is a bottomless black hole of bad times, dude.

It's weird. I had my doubts, but I am excited now. It feels like anything is possible. It feels like there's a reason to get up in the morning. It feels like I'm finally awake after sleepwalking for so long.

◆　◆　◆

Holy balls! Perhaps fortune favors the bold even harder than I thought. Last night I made up my mind to enter into the world according to Nick — without question a ballsy move. Well, that technically doesn't start until Friday, but I'm apparently already reaping the benefits of my newly declared boldness.

It went a little something like this.

I smushed some clay into a vague bowl shape for my ceramics project in art class. Beth is way better at art stuff than me, so she was already at the point of glazing her bowl. She slathered some goop onto her clay with a paint brush.

"What are you doing this weekend?"

I shrugged.

"Nothing really."

Beth rotated her bowl and applied more glaze.

"Wanna go to the movies or something?" she asked.

I played it cool. Thought about it for a minute.

"Sure."

Okay, that's a lie. I wasn't cool at all. When she asked me, I almost choked to death on my tongue I was trying to say "yes" so fast. I spit out a lot of gibberish-y syllables. Something like "Eeeeyeuhyuheyeyeuheyeyes. Yes."

She laughed, but not like she was laughing at me. Sometimes she looks at me when she laughs, and I know somehow that we are together. She even put her hand on my arm.

I don't want to read too much into things like that, though. I don't want to let my expectations get way out of control and set myself up for the biggest disappointment ever.

This is good, though. I mean, I'm not 100% clear on

whether or not she considers this a date, but I figure it has to be a step in the right direction regardless. She could ask any-goddamn-body to go to the movies with her. Six billion people on the planet. Any of them. She asked me.

The hardest part will be not hyperventilating to the point of passing out during the trailers and missing the movie. No, really, I've never had to be nervous around Beth before. I always thought I had no chance, so... But damn. I suddenly have everything to lose. I hope I don't screw this up.

Oh yeah. *Where are they now?* update on Troy Summers: Troy is on crutches now. I assume it's some kind of football-related injury. It's always tough to see a promising, young athlete sidelined like that, but I somehow found a way to hold back the tears. The real downside? If the injury was severe, I probably would have already heard about it. So he probably just sprained an ankle or something. Ah, well. Pretty funny to watch him hobble around in any case.

And back to the most important point: Beth asked me to the movies.

Boom.

CHAPTER 7

I WALKED TO NICK'S AFTER school. Talk radio blared from his apartment so loud I could hear it from a couple doors down. I climbed the staircase to their door, knocked and heard someone say to come in.

Walking through the kitchen, I could see Nick reading about Hare Krishnas on the green La-Z-Boy again. That seemed dumb. I didn't understand why he'd crank up the radio and read a book.

As I entered the living room, however, I saw Donnie leaned over an ancient stereo on the giant wooden spool they use as a coffee table. An unlit cigarette dangled from his lip. He shushed me as soon as I stepped into his view, even though I hadn't made any noise. He pointed at the radio. I took a second to actually listen and realized it wasn't talk radio. Donnie was listening to a police scanner.

"We've got a four-zero-six in progress on Lovell Street," Donnie hissed at me. He had crazy eyes.

"What's a four-zero-six?" I said. I felt the need to whisper, but I felt pretty stupid about it.

"A B-and-E, man," Donnie said. He read the blank expression on my face. "Breaking and entering. Jesus, kid."

"Oh..."

I scratched my chest even though it didn't itch.

"Where's Lovell Street?" I said.

Donnie's brow furrowed. He looked at Nick.

"Where is Lovell Street?" he said.

Nick didn't respond verbally. He rolled his eyes.

"I think it's up toward the Northside," Donnie said. His hands shot out to his sides like an umpire signaling safe. "Listen!"

Cops droned on with lots of codes I didn't know. Donnie shushed me again even though the scanner was the only noise in the room. I had always wondered who the people were that actually sat around listening to police scanners, and somehow Donnie totally made sense in that role.

Nick sighed and headed for the kitchen. I followed.

"Is he on drugs or something? His eyes look insane," I said. I talked in that gravelly register just above a whisper so Donnie wouldn't hear.

"What? Oh, I doubt it. He goes apeshit over the police scanner every couple months. Gets all manic and eventually asks me to hide it from him."

Nick scooped several spoonfuls of coffee into the machine while he talked.

"He can't handle it for some reason. I think it's the anticipation. Always waitin' to see what happens next. And it never ends. There's always another crime unfoldin' somewheres, you know? Somethin' about that sets him off. You want some coffee?"

"Huh? No."

Nick flipped the switch, and the coffee machine purred and dripped, suddenly wet with life.

"So I take it you has chosen the dark side."

"Wha... Oh, right. More lessons, yeah."

"Figured you would."

A loud gasp erupted in the other room, and Donnie ran into the kitchen. His feet thudded across the wood floor like the heads of sledgehammers.

"Four-eight-eight! Four-eight-eight in progress!" he said. "And it's no more than a mile from where we stand right now." White strings of goo fluttered in the corners of his mouth when he spoke. Froth.

"Calm down," Nick said, pouring some coffee. He looked at me. "That's a petty theft. Four-eight-eight."

Donnie lost interest with us and ran back to his precious scanner.

Nick scooted himself up to sit on the counter with his mug of black coffee in his hand. His feet dangled off the edge, which made him seem like a little kid.

"Tonight you leave the world you know."

He took a long sip from his mug.

◆　　◆　　◆

We parked outside of a public tennis court. It was dark now, and street lamps glowed high above us, but the houses along the rest of the block seemed to hide in the shadows under tall pine trees.

Nick handed me a pair of brown cloth gloves. I guess I just stared at them for a second while he slid his own on, so he finally said:

"For fingerprints."

Part of me wanted to protest, wanted to turn back, but I didn't. I'd made my choice. I chose this. I wanted this. Didn't I?

I put the gloves on. The fabric felt softer than I'd imagined.

56

It felt right.

He tied a black dew rag around his head and gave me a Corona Light baseball hat. I wore it backward. Not 'cause I was trying to look cool or anything. I have a triangular shaped face, so the bill of a baseball hat somehow makes me look like a weird banjo-playing hick or something. I hate it. Aviator sunglasses are a no-go as well.

Sigh.

Anyway, we crept out onto the sidewalk. It was the strangest feeling. I mean, Nick hadn't directly said what we were doing, but I knew it'd involve breaking and entering AKA a four-zero-six. I think it was so over-the-top absurd to me that I didn't even get as nervous as I probably should.

My limbs seemed far away and partially numb. It felt like walking around in a dream.

We circled behind a pale blue modular house and trudged through the Virginia creeper sprawling along the home's perimeter. Things progressed quickly from there.

Nick popped the screen out of a back window like he'd done it a million times before. He shined his small flashlight into the window and swung it around the room. It was quick, but I could make out a washer and dryer.

He pushed his face to my ear and whispered.

"When we get inside, just squat down and stay perfectly silent. Let your eyes and ears adjust. Then I will make the first move."

He pushed the bottom sash of the window up and hesitated for a moment. (Jesus! Remind me to lock my damn windows.) He turned off the flashlight and clenched it between his teeth, then he pulled himself up and disappeared headfirst into the opening. Aside from the faintest hiss of the window sliding open, all of his moves had been silent.

I pulled myself up, mimicking his headfirst motion. There is something very much insane about moving face-first into the pitch blackness of a foreign private residence. I felt like I was watching myself do it. I mean, I knew on some level that I was the one doing it, yet it was like it wasn't really me. Like some important part of me had just shut down, but the rest was somehow still going.

I leaned forward into the darkness. My hands stretched out into black nothing before eventually touching on the cool linoleum floor. I eased my way in and kneeled down like he said. My jeans rustled a bit as they slid over the window sill, and it reminded me of the sound of a fingernail scraping dried food off of denim, but other than that I kept everything pretty quiet.

Apart from the crickets outside, I couldn't hear or see anything. It's weird how quickly deprivation (and adrenaline) sharpen the senses.

So the first thing I sensed upon settling inside was the stench of cat piss. Yep. Kitty litter, dude. Cat whiz possesses a certain tang that is very recognizable no matter the circumstances. Eventually I also detected a few notes of some kind of liquid laundry detergent odor.

Nick touched my shoulder to let me know he was kneeling to my right. We squatted there for what seemed like an hour. A couple of times I got a little panicky, but it went away as fast as it came upon me. I sometimes felt like maybe I was breathing loud.

It wasn't until I wiped the back of my wrist across my brow

that I realized I was soaked with sweat. That seemed weird. Like I was physically panicking, but the me part had mostly stayed numb to it or something. Maybe that's what courage is sometimes, though. Being too overwhelmed to even feel the fear.

Something poked the side of my neck and worked its way up to my ear. Fingers. Nick grabbed the back of my head so he could find his way to lean in and whisper again.

"I'll go check it out. Wait here."

My eyes had adjusted enough now that I could somewhat sense him moving away from me, a faintly darker black moving through the rest of the black, but that was about it. (How many shades of black can there really be?)

I waited. My heart hammered in my chest. Blood throbbed through my veins. I sat in this dark dream world in a cloud of kitty piss. (You'd think you might get used to the cat pee smell eventually, but I did not.) And I realized this was exciting, hiding here in some stranger's house. That it might be the most exciting thing I'd ever done. Life pumped through me like it never had before. When you're a kid everyone tells that you anything is possible, and that you can do anything you truly want and all that shit. This was the first time in my life that I felt in my gut that anything was possible. Anything.

The sound of footsteps thumped outside the room. Loud. Hard. No attempt to conceal themselves. And they were getting closer. I pictured a large bald man wearing a navy blue bathrobe and sporting a double-barreled shotgun.

"It's all clear."

It was Nick. The beam from his flashlight danced into the room and blinded me for a second before he twirled it away

59

from my eyes.

"No one is home. Come on out."

I walked out toward the circle of light shining down on beige Berber carpet in the hallway. Nick smirked.

"We mighta picked a dud, man. Not lookin' good."

I followed him into a bedroom.

"Here."

He handed me the flashlight. I shined it on an oak dresser while he pulled the drawers out one by one and dumped them on the floor. Once or twice he stooped to sift through the pile at his feet, but he didn't find anything of interest.

"What about the TV?" I said, gesturing to the dresser top. "It's got to be worth something."

Nick sighed.

"First of all, that shit is from about 1998. Second of all, are you goin' to discretely lug that monster out of here?"

"Oh. Yeah, that's a good point."

"Come on."

We strode out into the kitchen. He opened the fridge and surveyed the scene a while. After a long moment, he grabbed a block of cheddar and took a huge bite out of it. He chewed in silence a moment before our eyes met and this all became very amusing to him. He burst into a laughing fit. We're talking full-on spit-flying, crazy-eyed, mental hospital style giggle fest. That's the thing about Nick. He doesn't laugh very often, but once something gets him started, he has a hard time stopping.

He kept laughing as he flung the contents of a couple kitchen drawers onto the floor, silverware and cutlery crashing and clanging everywhere. I guess I kind of zoned out for a second as he kept at it, but the next thing I knew he had gone from laughing to screaming.

"Where is it!"

He scooped up a handful of butter knives and spoons and hurled them in the general direction of the microwave and coffee machine.

"Where's all the good shit!"

His breath heaved through clenched teeth. I don't know if I've ever seen anyone more angry. There was an entitled quality — almost like a whine — to his shouting that reminded me of a toddler, except if toddlers were like violent, filthy, full grown man-beasts or something.

He chucked things around a bit more. The toaster flew. The coffee carafe shattered. The potato masher skittered across the ceramic tiles.

Finally he just jumped straight up and down and reached under the bandana to clench two fistfuls of his hair.

Several full-throated screams rolled out of him. No words. Just primal screams. Seriously. Most ridiculous tantrum ever. It kind of freaked me out.

And just like that he went dead silent. His arm darted out and up to open a small cabinet above the fridge. He tossed a dishwasher manual aside, and ran his fingertips along the shelf bottom. His hand emerged holding a bracelet and a second sweep turned up a ring.

He tossed his head back and laughed.

"Gold."

His eyes locked with mine, and he looked about as crazy as Donnie with the scanner. The word "euphoric" seems right. It rarely does, I'd say. It's not like I'm over here just tossing "euphoric" around left and right or something.

"Every time. I fuckin' knew it! If the jewelry ain't in the bedroom, it's in the kitchen."

On the ride home he elaborated on all of this. We drove around the weird suburbs outside of town. Row after row of identical box houses.

"It's all about attention to detail. Do you know how I knew which window to pick?"

I thought about it.

"Nope."

"Because I saw the dryer vent. A laundry room is just about the perfect point of entry. That shit is always vacant, and it's usually got stuff like a furnace or water heater that would make any of my noises less suspicious."

That made sense.

"You don't seem to make any noises," I said. "You're like a damn ninja."

He smirked.

"And why do you think I picked the blue house instead of the nicer lookin' yella house next door or the big brick house across the street?"

I didn't bother to actually think about it this time.

"I don't know. Why?"

He flicked the ash off the tip of his cigarette out the Malibu's window and brought the smoldering tube back to his lips.

"The yella house had a security alarm sticker in the front window. Coulda been a fake, of course, or their subscription to ADT could be expired or whatever, but it don't really matter. It ain't worth the trouble in any case. The brick house had a dog pen off to the side. Again, we don't know the details, but we don't need to. Why mess with the possibility of a Rottweiler when we don't have to?"

"So why the kitchen?"

"Huh?"

"The jewelry. You said if it's not in the bedroom, it's in the kitchen."

"Ah. Right. Well, I can't say for sure, you know, but my theory is that they are plannin' to sell it. I mean, if it's like a treasured ring, you keep it in a jewel box in your bedroom, right? Like if it's a luxury item or whatever you want to call it. But if you're thinkin' about pawnin' it, it becomes a utilitarian item. Your main concern now is that you don't want to misplace it, so you put it in the room with all of the other useful items — the kitchen."

I nodded.

"Weird."

"I guess if it was a man, he might even put it in the garage, but men don't really have all that much jewelry, you know?"

His voice trailed off now, like he was lost in an imaginary garage full of Rolexes and gold chains or something.

He swept his arm in front of the windshield, gesturing to the cul-de-sac around us like those perpetually smiling women on the Price is Right revealing a set of designer sofas.

"See all that? All these boxes is just settin' there. Waitin'. Waitin' for us to come along and take all the shiny shit out of them."

He smiled.

I gazed out at the modular homes and tried to imagine how he must see them, like rows of presents waiting under the tree. Each one full of surprises. Like the whole world was just waiting to be explored. Plundered. Like he was just going to take whatever he wanted from it and nobody could stop him.

"Do you kind of get it now?" he said. "How they teach you to feel powerless when you could do anything? How they want to tell you about what's right and wrong and make you feel all small?"

"I think so."

"There ain't no right or wrong. None of it means nothin'. There is just things that happen."

We turned onto a dirt road cutting through a cornfield. Everything went silent aside from the periodic tinks of tiny rocks hitting the car.

"Out of all of the trillions of years of the Earth's history, you might be alive for one 70 or 80 year period. That ain't so long. You should be out ready to burn this motherfucker to the groun' while you can. But they somehow get you all scared and hung up on these stupid ideas."

I didn't know what to say, so the car fell silent again.

"I don't know. I am tryin' to show you how I see it. Expand your horizons and shit. I mean, Jesus, we all buy clothes made by kids in Chinese sweatshops. People in Africa starve to death. The people in power must know there is no right or wrong to let those things happen. It only matters to them when it serves to keep you feelin' powerless and small and scared so they can keep order and keep makin' money."

He flicked his cigarette butt out the window and lit another.

"When we drop bombs on people, that is good. When other people drop bombs on us or blow shit up, that is evil. It's all a joke. It ain't real."

He turned to face me.

"Couldn't you feel it? Didn't you feel that when we were in that house?"

"Yeah."

I think I did.

CHAPTER 8

JUST GOT BACK FROM THE movies with Beth. I think it went pretty well. I don't know.

We loaded up on snacks. We're talking a huge tub of popcorn, slathered in butter or whatever the hell hydrogenated oil fake butter stuff they have. (Trans fats? Dr. Oz would never approve.) To drink, a large Coke for me — no ice — and a medium Sunkist for the lady. (That's the orange stuff.) In terms of candy, I went for gummy bears and Twix, also known as the best of both worlds. She went for Tropical Berry Skittles. She could've had anything. Tropical Berry Skittles. Her choice.

We were pretty early, so we sat a while in the mostly empty theater while dated trivia questions popped up on the screen. Bruce Willis this. John Travolta that. The floor was all sticky as usual. I kind of think it'd be weird if the floor wasn't sticky, actually. Like some piece of theater tradition would be missing.

"Girls are so insane," she said.

"Oh, really?" I said. "I guess I don't really know about it."

There weren't a bunch of people there, but she was talking loud enough that I felt kind of uncomfortable. It was weird. On one hand, I could appreciate the idea that she was comfortable or confident enough to just let it rip, but on the other hand, talking that loud in public is almost like an act of aggression. Sort of like a "Yeah, I see you sitting over there, dude, and I'm going to just yell anyway, so fuck off," kind of thing.

"Well, you're lucky," she continued. "One on one, maybe

they aren't so bad. When you get a group of girls together, though, they suddenly morph into these psychotic, cutthroat control freaks. It's all a very unsavory business."

"Sounds like it."

I wanted to ask about the specifics, but I felt weird. Plus I was kind of just hoping that she would stop yelling, you know?

"Women are obsessed with control. Just trust me on this."

I shoved a fistful of popcorn into my mouth and nodded. She followed suit.

Before the movie even started, my stomach kinda hurt from pounding down all that junk food. Beth ate like a champ, though. She powered through the Skittles, put a real dent on the popcorn and even had some of my gummy bears and Twix. She plowed it right down long after I felt sick. Pretty impressive, really.

Eventually the theater went dark and the trailers and movie started. I didn't know if I was supposed to like hold her hand or something. So I was kind of thinking about that the whole time, and I didn't pay attention to the actual movie so much. My palms got all sweaty, so I kept drying them off in case I ever got up the courage to make contact.

I didn't.

About forty minutes in, Beth got up and went to the bathroom for a super long time. When she got back, she smelled like peppermint and offered me a Tic Tac. That is like the only plot point I remember from the evening. Except a few minutes after that, she put her hand on my arm again, like she did in art class. She only left it there for a few seconds, but I don't know. It made me not feel as weird or gross or whatever.

As far as the actual movie, I do remember that there was a

scene in there where a couple of the guys had to pee really bad from drinking too much iced tea. The dummies in the theater were loving it. So yeah. It was that kind of movie.

Also — side note — I hate how pretentious people have to always say "film" instead of "movie" in their stupid la-de-da voices. No one cares that you watched some movie, dickface. We don't think you're super cool and sophisticated and shit. So there.

◆　◆　◆

In Psychology today we learned about this study on brain activity when playing video games. The book had these photos of a brain scan with like a rainbow of colors in the head, the areas with brighter colors representing a lot of activity in that part of the brain, you know.

So when someone is first playing a particular Xbox game or whatever, their whole brain is lit up red and yellow. Like because they have to learn how the game works and all of that, the whole thing is engaged and figuring it out.

Once they've played the game a bunch of times, though, only the two or three areas of the brain necessary for that particular task light up. Seriously maybe like 1/5 of the scan was now lit up in a couple of little spots. Most of it was black — completely inactive. I guess that's why games get old after a while. Once something becomes routine, most of your brain can just shut down, you know.

It made me think about how my mom has this daily ritual of going to work, coming home, making food, watching TV, going to bed and starting the same thing again the next day. So it's like most of her brain can just sleep all day. It seems like a lot of adults are like that, really.

♦   ♦   ♦

I had a dream last night that I was sitting on the couch, but I could fly around the house if I tucked my knees up against my chest. It was rad. I think I must have been faintly conscious of the fact that I was lying motionless in real life or something.

Beth was there, and her cat kept dying and coming back to life. This fat tabby cat named Geoff. It would just slump over on my desk and die. And she'd get all upset and start crying. And time would pass, like a few days. And we'd talk about how we should probably bury him 'cause he might start smelling or whatever. And then I'd touch him, to pick him up to go bury him, you know, and he'd suddenly roll over and be fine. It happened three or four times over the course of the dream. She said that it must just be a dislocated shoulder.

At the end I went outside and floated way up above my house. Not our apartment now, but the house from when I was little. Anyway, I went up past this telephone pole by the garage and just kept going. And then finally I kind of stopped going up and just hovered way up there a while, looking down on the house and the back yard and everything. I could see Beth sleeping on a porch swing, and Nick and Tammie fighting in the driveway. It all looked so small. And I thought about how eventually I'd have to fall down or something.

♦   ♦   ♦

Remember all that talk about McDonald's advertising? How they want to be your trusted friend and everything?

Well, whatever they're doing with those ads, it works, apparently. To an insane degree, it works.

I read about a study today that found that kids think food in a McDonald's wrapper tastes better. And the food inside the wrapper, you ask? Doesn't actually matter.

The power of that McDonald's branding is so strong, the messages in those relentless ads wired so deeply in the impressionable young brains, that they prefer the food in the McDonald's wrapper no matter what it is. If they're given two servings of the exact same food — one in a McDonald's wrapper and the other in a plain wrapper — they think the McDonald's food tastes better the vast majority of the time. The same McDonald's fries won preference 77% to 13% as to tasting better, with the remaining 10% saying they tasted the same. Even with stuff like store bought milk and carrots, the kids preferred the McDonald's wrapped version. (They liked the ones labeled McMilk and McCarrots, I guess.)

The Stanford researcher who conducted the study, Dr. Tom Robinson, said the kids' perception of taste was "physically altered by the branding."

Yes, you read that correctly.

Physically.

Altered.

Well played yet again.

CHAPTER 9

LESSON THREE TRANSPIRED THIS EVENING. So I'm supposed to feel smarter, I guess, but I feel dumber. Let me start at the beginning, though.

I went to Nick's after school. No crazy police scanner stuff this time. Donnie was away assembling tacos. (That's the official terminology they use at Taco Bell. "Assembling tacos," I mean. For real.)

Nick sat in the living room, trimming his fingernails with a pocket knife. Tammie sprawled next to him, still wearing her pajamas. She painted her toenails, alternating pink and black.

Tammie looked up from her nails and brushed the hair out of her eyes with the back of her hand.

"Hi."

"Hey," I said.

Nick didn't even bother looking up when I first walked in. He looked distracted. After he was finished with his lumberjack manicure, he sprang from his chair and jogged toward his bedroom.

"Oh, wait here a minute," he said.

When he came back, he had a wad of money in his hand. He peeled four 50-dollar bills and a 20 from the stack and handed them to me.

"What's this?" I said.

I fanned the money out in front of me like a hand of cards.

"It's your cut."

"My cut?"

"From the other night. I sold that jewelry. This is your cut."

"Oh."

"Look, I ain't goin' to lie to ya. I didn't split it 50-50 or nothin'. We both know I did most of the work and all. But you were there, and people who work should get paid, right? So that's your payment."

"Thanks. It's just... I mean, it seems like a lot."

"Gold ain't no joke."

"Yeah. Sheesh."

He shoved the wad of money into his pocket and we sat down.

"Tonight's an easy one."

"Huh?"

I was still a little shook up by the whole money thing, I guess, so I didn't have a clue what he was talking about.

"The next lesson."

"Oh, right."

"Your task? To procure alcohol."

I paused a beat to let it sink in.

"That's it? But couldn't I just have you buy it for me?"

"Nope. And Donnie ain't here, but even if he was, I wouldn't let him buy it for you neither."

I thought about that. I knew Tammie was only 19, so she would be a no-go as well.

"So what am I supposed to do?"

"Acquire the alcoholic beverage of your choice."

"Well, yeah, I grasped that. I meant how?"

"Don't matter to me. Be resourceful."

"Great."

Keep in mind that I've never been drunk, of course. I believe we touched on the thing about me being a huge pussy already, but, honestly, I cannot stress that enough.

"Better git," Nick said. "You ain't gonna find any booze sittin' around here."

When I got out to the porch, Tammie was there. Like she was waiting for me. She smiled.

"Don't worry about it," she whispered. "All you have to do is wait outside the store and ask someone to buy you some beer. It's really simple, and it totally works."

"So you've done this?"

"Loads of times."

She kind of put her arm around my shoulder and did like a sideways hug thing. I guess it did make me feel a little better.

Shit. I can't keep my eyes open. I'll have to finish this tomorrow.

◆　◆　◆

I left Nick's and walked a few blocks down to Broad Street Market, a small grocery store that mostly specializes in liquor sales. There's a little three-walled porch area by the front doors, bricks painted maroon, and there's a rectangular opening crafted into one of the walls like maybe a window was there once. Kids sit on the ledge in that opening often, and I sat there now, facing the parking lot. My legs dangled over the brick wall, and I could just reach the tips of my toes to the pavement and kick at rocks. Something nice about the sound of my rubber soles scraping rocks over blacktop.

It was Friday night, so the parking lot buzzed with people

from all walks of life preparing to binge drink. College kids. Factory workers. Business people. Everyone knows that the weekend is generally a time to funnel hooch into your face until you pass out, puke or both.

The crowd provided a gift and a curse for my purposes. On one hand, lots of people meant lots of opportunities to ask one of them to buy me beer. On the other hand, a constant flow of customers made it harder for me to single any of them out for a private, one-on-one conversation. Would people grow more reluctant to buy a 40-ounce of King Cobra for a high school kid if they knew others were watching and listening? My guess was abso-friggin-lutely.

(And yeah, I did choose King Cobra primarily because of the cool cobra on the bottle. It's also very reasonably priced. Bonus.)

So I waited. And I debated what characteristics my target demographic should possess. The first segment of the population I ruled out was older women. Moms (and grandmas) are probably the lowest probability group in terms of converting a purchase of teenage booze. Don't misread that. I know there are loads of trashy grandmas that would love nothing more than to furnish me with malt liquor. We're speaking in terms of probabilities, though. The trashy grandmas are outnumbered.

A non-trashy mom hopped out of a green dodge caravan and smiled at me on her way into the store, her natural kindness and decency illustrating my point.

Next, I ruled out anyone wearing business attire. Suits, khakis, polo shirts — no, no, no. Neckties? Don't make me chuckle. Casual dress only, please. Camo anything would be considered a perk.

A man sporting a pin-striped suit stepped out of a Lexus and slid on expensive sunglasses for the 20-foot walk to the store. Based on nothing more than years of TV viewing, I felt somehow certain he would be purchasing scotch.

Anyway, I realized that I was stalling. All of these demographic thoughts served as a way to put off actually asking someone, which I admit intimidated my balls off.

I started thinking about what words I would use, testing out possibilities in my imagination:

"Hi. Can I get you to buy me some beer?"

"Hey. Could you buy me alcohol?"

"Will you buy me a forty of King Cobra?"

"Pardon. Would you do me the small service of purchasing an ice cold lager that I might imbibe this eve?"

Somehow I liked the idea of jumping right into the question and being specific up front. A hard lead loaded with the facts. No fluff. No needless words. All that. No more pussyfooting. Whoever walked up next was going to get asked.

So of course the parking lot died. Not a soul for miles. I felt like a damn tumbleweed should roll by.

Thinking back, I'm not sure if the place actually got less busy or if time seemed to slow down 'cause I was dying of nervousness.

Finally, a guy in a black t-shirt and baseball hat walked up. Now, technically, his hat wasn't camo — it was plain black — but it did have the mesh trucker-style in the back, which is a fine camo substitute in my book. I hopped off my perch and moved quickly to meet him a good five or ten paces away from the store.

I planted my feet, and I blasted him with my question:

"Will you buy me a forty of King Cobra?"

Nailed it.

FUCKING.

NAILED IT.

I thrust money toward him. He half-flinched when my hand moved toward his person and then stopped dead in his tracks and seemed to size me up. His eyes squinted as he looked me over as though in deep concentration. It seemed like forever. I felt like music from an old Clint Eastwood movie should be playing.

"King Cobra?" he said.

His voice sounded like sandpaper coated with nicotine and whiskey stains.

"Yes, sir," I said. (Sir. A nice touch.)

He nodded, creases forming at the corners of his mouth. The creases slowly curled up into a half-smile as he took my money.

"Meet me in the alley out back."

"Sure."

I wasn't exactly sure what he was talking about, 'cause there are kind of two alleys running along different sides of the building, really, but I went for the closer one. Upon reaching the alley, I realized that this would be a great way to steal my money. Here in the alley, I had no view of the front door or much of anything beyond the brick walls surrounding me. He could just buy a lot of beef jerky and Skoal and head for the hills, laughing his dumb face off all the while.

It felt like forever. I tried to stay all cool and calm, but half of me was thinking this guy just stole my $20, and the other half was sure I was going to somehow get arrested for this. I kept counting to ten and telling myself that if I got to ten and he still wasn't there, I'd go check it out. But instead when I got to ten, I'd just start over, saying to myself that I really meant it this time.

Finally, he strutted around the corner with a brown bag in one hand and a pile of money in the other. He smiled as he approached.

"Here you go," he rasped.

He dumped the change into my hands and then handed over the concealed elixir. The money was all there. He didn't even keep a buck or two for his troubles.

"Thank you."

"Not a problem, bucko."

(Bucko? This was new to me.)

He pivoted and walked off into the sunset. It's somehow comforting to know that, even in this day and age, there are still good Samaritans out there willing to buy beer for strange underage kids for no good reason. To me, those are the real heroes.

◆　◆　◆

I headed back to Nick's with the secret potion hidden in the bag and nestled in my arm like a premature infant. I had to really work to stay in G-mode.

The nerves bound up into a weird clenching fist in my gut, and I wanted to swivel my head around constantly to make sure the cops weren't tailing me. G-mode required me to instead mosey along like all was normal and, if anything, a little boring.

There are only a few blocks between the store and Nick's, but it was Friday night and getting toward the whole evening rush deal, so traffic was much heavier now. Minivans and sedans rushed past. I forced myself to maintain eye contact with the sidewalk, but the sound of every passing vehicle still made my heart stop. (My heart is a wuss. Duh.) The only other thing that stood out during the walk was the smell of freshly cut grass.

It wasn't until I arrived at the safety of Nick's that I sort of said to myself, "Oh, I'm probably going to have to actually drink this or whatever now." It really hadn't crossed my mind. I guess it's difficult to plan too far ahead when you're busy imagining yourself shitting your pants while cops cuff you and haul you in and all of that. So yeah...

I strode into the living room and unsheathed the bottle of King Cobra, except it wasn't the black and gold label of a bottle of King Cobra staring back at me. It was a thinner bottle of pale pink liquid. The label had a farm and huge berries and stuff all over it. I read it. Strawberry Hill flavored Boone's Farm.

"Awww," Donnie said, still sporting his Taco Bell attire. "Look how cute."

He and Nick found this ultra-hilarious, which I guess it was pretty funny or whatever, but... Tammie didn't laugh, though I could tell by the strained look on her face that she wanted to. She was holding off for my sake.

"I asked the guy to get me a forty of King Cobra," I said, but I think they were laughing too hard to notice. Whatever.

I wanted malt liquor, but instead I got this fake wine. I cracked it open anyway. By "cracked it open" I really mean "unscrewed the cap" and, from what I understand, the screw top is the ultimate sign of class and quality in the wine world. It smelled like a goddamn fruit salad mixed with perfume or something, except all artificial fruit. (The perfume was real.)

I tipped the bottle back and took a swig. The words "sickeningly" and/or "cloyingly" sweet really do not do this stuff justice. It is beyond all of that. It is like drinking artificial strawberry syrup with a dash of Ax Body Spray for its rich aromatic quality.

"I'm just glad you got this Boone's Farm in time for your sweet sixteen," Donnie said. He was a real barrel of laughs all of a sudden.

All I wanted to do was chug down this Boone's Farm and be done with it, but it's basically impossible to chug something so sweet. The best you can kind of do is kind of sip it and try not to retch. So I watched Donnie and Nick play video games and kept nursing my drink. As I got toward the bottom of the bottle, it was a little warmer and that much harder to get down.

"Almost polished 'er off," Donnie said, grinning. "So are you fuckin' wasted, or what?"

"No," I said. More than anything else, my face was hot.

"Bullshit!" he said. "You're sloshed!"

"No, I'm not. Watch."

To demonstrate how not- drunk I was, I hopped down onto the floor and started doing pushups. (Made sense at the time. I think I thought my perfect form would speak for itself or something.)

Donnie and Nick howled with laughter. Tears streamed down Tammie's face, she was laughing so damn hard.

"You're, like, way drunker than I thought," Donnie said.

Nick just laughed that kind of hissing laugh through his teeth.

I don't know. I didn't think I was drunk, but I must have been. I don't get what all the fuss is about, to be honest. My face felt all hot, and I guess I felt a little dumber than normal. Not much of a lesson.

I slammed the rest of it down and felt a little sick before long. I think it was more from the sweetness than the alcohol.

Donnie went to bed kind of early 'cause he had to work in the morning, and Tammie fell asleep on the loveseat, so before too long it was just me and Nick. He was out of cigarettes, so he was using Donnie's machine to roll a shitty one.

"So what do you think of your first drunk experience?" he said.

"Not much."

He smiled.

"Didn't care for it, eh? It ain't for everyone."

"What's the point?"

The machine popped as he pulled the lever to pack the tobacco into the tube. He pulled free the final product and lit it before responding.

"If you mean, why do people drink in a sorta general way…"

"I mean for me. What's the point of making me drink? What wisdom am I supposed to glean from this?"

He chuckled.

"Well, there ain't no wisdom in it. It ain't about that. Life don't really work the way they make you think in school. I can't teach you some simple lesson and have that somehow prepare you for what the world is really like. I can only try to show you by having you experience different things for yourself and seein' what you think of them."

He tapped the cigarette in the glass ashtray on the armrest of his chair.

"I think alcohol is a pretty basic way to do two things. First, to break down all the bullshit propaganda that tries to make you scared. I mean, alcohol can be dangerous, of course, but think about what you're experiencin' right now compared to all of the fear-mongerin' stuff they've pumped you full of in school. Complete nonsense."

I nodded.

"The second thing is a little more abstract. I wanted you to try something that would alter your state. Now, you might not even realize it just yet, and booze is one of the subtler ways to do it, I'll admit. Since it's your first time, and you only had one bottle of girly stuff, you might not feel like your brain is working all that differently, but it is. I think there's a lot to learn from that. Maybe it's different for everyone, but having your thoughts affected can give you a sort of perspective into how flawed and warped your perceptions can be. And it definitely ain't somethin' that I could just teach you. You have to do it and feel it on your own."

Just then, the cherry fell off the tip of his cigarette and quickly burned a black smudge into the rug. Nick licked the tips of his fingers and pinched it to extinguish it.

"Shit. Don't tell Donnie about that," he said and scooted the recliner over the black mark.

CHAPTER 10

WE TALKED ABOUT THE LEFT and right brain today in Psychology. I guess everyone kind of knows the gist: the left brain is orderly, logical, rational, organizational, controls language (mostly). The right brain is chaotic, emotional, passionate, creative, intuitive. I guess the super simple way to summarize it is that the left brain thinks and the right brain feels.

I think the thing that seemed most interesting to me is that the communication between them isn't great. So there's basically all of this stuff going on in your right brain that you are only vaguely aware of. All of these instincts and emotions and impulses bubbling up all the time but always just out of the reach of your conscious mind.

The professor told this story about Agatha Christie, this ancient mystery writer. She was sort of aware of how her right brain needed time to cook up the endings to these stories she was working on, so she'd take baths. She would soak and just let her mind go clear. Let it wander. And so long as her right brain sort of had some space to work, she'd come up with these new twists and turns that would snap perfectly into place in a satisfying way. Like she knew that her imagination always wanted to find the perfect solution to the problem, and it just needed time without her left brain cluttering everything up.

So here's where it gets real crazy. Some people have epilepsy so bad that they have to sever the part of the brain that connects the left and right hemisphere. Once that baby is cut, everything gets a little funky. The two halves of the brain can't communicate and there are all kinds of weird repercussions. My favorite was "Alien Hand Syndrome." Basically some of the people with severed hemispheres could still feel things in their non-dominant hand, but it would move purposefully without them controlling it. In other words, a right-handed guy would witness his left hand grab a hairbrush off the table and start brushing his hair without him choosing to do so.

They get all weirded out by it, which I guess makes sense. But I think I get it. Your right brain controls your left hand, so if you see the brush and your right brain gets the impulse to brush your hair, it does so. The problem is that your left brain doesn't know about it since the sides are split, and that's sort of the conscious part of you, so it feels like your hand has a mind of its own. Weird shit in any case.

Another set of tests they did on the differences in the left and right brain that I thought was interesting involved like injecting stuff to numb one side or the other of the brain. So even though I kind of crudely summed things up earlier, every individual brain is a little different, right? Like 95% of right-handed people have their speech center mostly on their left side. Obviously that leaves the other 5% as oddballs with their speech mostly wired and coming from their right brain. (For the record, around 70% of left-handed people still have their language function dominated by their left brain.) They do this test to numb one side or the other to sort of find out what areas are dominant for different skills for that individual.

So they inject this stuff, and as it takes effect a lot of the patients begin to shiver. The people with their speech completely dominant in their left brain can't speak or even comprehend language with their left brain numbed. But — and this is the awesome part — they can still sing songs, with the proper lyrics and everything, because music is usually centered in the right brain.

Fucking mind-blowing.

♦　♦　♦

We decided to go to this pasta place. Beth and me, I mean. Pasta Pasta. That's the name of the restaurant. It's this somewhat fancy pasta bar, which probably sounds like an impossible combination, but that's what it is, so fuck you. So like you order a type of pasta and then go to this little sauce buffet type situation and ladle on various sauces.

Yep. I don't know.

It felt the most like our first real date yet, so I was extra nervous. I didn't know if I should sit next to her or across from her. I went with the latter, but I regretted it at once. The table was kind of big, so she was like really far away from me.

"Ooh… I think I'm going for this one," Beth said. "These little lasagna wraps."

She pointed to a photo of them on the menu. They did look pretty tasty.

"Isn't there like meat and stuff inside there?" I said.

She read the menu closer. It said "stuffed with a spicy sausage blend," which, it occurred to me, would also be a particularly disgusting way to describe a girl in an orgy.

"Yeah, I guess so," she said. "Hm… I think I'm getting them anyway."

Classic mistake.

Our table sat smack in the middle of the floor, so we were fenced in by idiots. It was even worse 'cause my back was up against a table of douchey frat guys. They all looked vaguely like Dane Cook, which made me assume right away that they weren't very funny. It also made me feel vulnerable somehow to have them lurking around behind me.

I didn't know what the hell to order. My gut leaned toward regular old spaghetti. I figured, why mess with success? Plus this sauce bar would provide the real star of the dish, right?

A family of really short people with stubby little legs screened our view of the buffet, so we couldn't make out any saucy details. This helped the meal maintain an aura of mystery, at least, I guess.

Oh, also I wore this kind of fancier yellow button up shirt that I've never worn before. So I felt dumb. Yep.

The waitress came to take our orders. I think she was laughing at me 'cause I was being so awkward and sitting like a mile away from Beth and everything. Not laughing in a mean way or anything. Laughing in an "Aww, that's cute. What an awkward first date!" kinda way. But it's weird 'cause I didn't really feel any awkwardness between me and Beth. I felt awkwardness at being out in public, fixing to eat food surrounded by strangers with stubby legs and such.

That seemed important somehow. Usually I feel the awkwardness from all sides. I actually felt close to Beth despite the physical distance between us.

Anyway, I thought long and hard about these cheese-stuffed ravioli guys. But I ultimately went for the spaghetti.

We had to wait behind these hippie dudes who clearly pried

themselves away from their hacky sack just long enough to take for-fucking-ever at the sauce bar. Eventually they dreadlocked out of our way, and the suspense was finally over. Only a sneeze guard stood between us and six stainless steel tubs of sauce.

First was a watery marinara loaded with dark chunks of sausage. Second was a watery marinara loaded with light and dark chunks of sausage. Third was a watery marinara loaded with three shades of sausage. Fourth was a white sauce. Fifth was a watery marinara loaded with light chunks of sausage and some mushrooms. Sixth was a watery marinara loaded with light and medium chunks of sausage.

"Christ," Beth said. "Am I supposed to ladle chunks of sausage over my sausage-stuffed pasta?"

I shrugged.

"You could go for the whi-"

She interrupted me.

"Don't even say it. Lasagna with white sauce is for pussies."

Indeed.

She was really mad.

"Ridiculous! They should probably change the name of this place to 'Sausage Sausage!'" she said.

I laughed. I kind of wanted to say something to somehow make things better, but maybe there are no words that can rectify a sausage party debacle such as this.

I actually calmed down and had fun after that. The food was awful, but we made fun of it together.

♦   ♦   ♦

"I missed it," Robert said.

"It's alright," I said. I kept my voice low so the other kids couldn't hear. "We're still up by three. Two more points and we win."

He scooped the badminton racquet under the shuttlecock and flipped it up toward me. I caught it and hit it over the net to our opponents Mike and Doug.

Wait. Opponents is not a strong enough word. Whatever is the plural of nemesis.

Eight badminton courts occupied the gym floor. Red electrical tape marked out precise boundaries around each net. This was the badminton tournament that wrapped up our two-week section on racquet sports.

There would be no "guesstimating" or lenience now. Maybe earlier in the week, during the lighthearted exhibition contests, people might let some things slide, but not today. Not in a tournament game. If that shit hit one millimeter outside of the red tape, it was out. Score it. Move on. First team to 21 wins the game, best two out of three games takes the match. Let's go.

Doug served a line drive shot that Robert returned with a snap of a backhand. The return floated a little, which gave Mike time to set up for a big overhand slam. He wound up and drilled it about as fast as you can hit a shuttlecock. Somehow I dug it out with an uppercut of a shot. I don't know how. It was too fast to even see and headed almost straight down, but I just did it without thinking. Like a reflex.

So here's the thing: I am fucking awesome at badminton. It might even be contagious or something, because Robert is pretty good, too. We mowed through the other teams to get to this championship match with Mike and Doug. We shut out a team of two goth girls, Jamie and Nicole, in back-to-back games to get warmed up. Next we crushed a slacker and a computer nerd, Ricky and Jeff. Two guys from the baseball team, Dirk and Jessie, gave us some competition, but no real trouble. We won those games 21-15 and 21-17 instead of the blowouts from our earlier matches.

My save of Mike's slam popped way up, so Doug drifted back a few steps to circle under it. He hit another line drive. Robert reached straight up and tapped it with the softest touch. Its rotation stopped, and it died in the air like a knuckleball. It made it just onto their side of the net and fell too fast for either of them to return. The shuttlecock hit the ground tip first and fell motionless onto its side.

Our serve again, thank you kindly.

"Shit," Mike said through clenched teeth.

Doug scowled. I think, but can't be sure, that it irks him more when Robert scores on them.

Mike and Doug were two of the best athletes at our school from little league to present. Mike was an All Valley running back. Doug was a starting wide receiver. They were also two of the more cruel of Troy's minions. One time Doug even got ejected from a game for twisting a guy's leg in the pile to try to break his ankle. So clearly these guys weren't into the whole "it doesn't matter if you win or lose, it's how you play the game" thing.

Maybe that was why I wanted to beat them so badly. Isn't that the natural urge here? To find a way to grind the sadistic kid's head into the ground so he can see what it feels like? I don't know how much of this kind of social nuance Robert understands, but he really wanted to beat them, too. Maybe more than me. He was getting pretty tense, actually, so I felt like I needed to keep him loose.

I reached out my racquet toward him side arm, and we did three low racquet fives followed by simultaneously flinging our racquet arms up in a kind of limp way. This was our handshake. I felt like this ritual was helping to keep him calm.

"Nice shot," I said, tipping the shuttlecock to him. "It's your serve."

He wiped the back of his wrist over his forehead, smearing sweat around more than anything else.

Mike and Doug were much better than the others we had faced. They were both quick and really aggressive. The velocity on their shots impressed everyone. The birdie hissed, they hit it with such ferocity.

It took us a game to adjust to the speed, I think. They won the first one 21-16. We rebounded, though, with a 21-14 win. I think they assumed they had us and let up a little bit. Their brows hadn't unfurrowed since then, and we were deep into Game 3 now.

Robert served. Doug returned. I smashed one. Mike saved it. It went back and forth like that rapidly now. Everyone was going all out. I blasted some line drives in hard-to-return spots, but someone always made it there just in time. I had to retreat and field a couple over my shoulder as well. Looking back, I don't know how I do some of this stuff. It's like I stop thinking and just go do it.

Finally Robert got in another of his soft touch shots, which Mike dove for and popped up. I smashed it right back down just shy of his sprawled figure. That made it 20-17.

"We're one point away," I said to Robert.

He smiled.

"This is it," he said.

Doug hit the birdie back over the net, and I slapped it across the wood floor toward Robert. He stooped to pick it up, and when he stood, he seemed to pause in thought a moment, twirling the shuttlecock in his fingers.

"This is it," he said again.

Everything got really quiet as Robert arched his back and moved to serve the match point.

"Alright, time to pack up the gear and get changed," the gym teacher, Mr. Smith, bellowed. Gym teachers don't talk. They bellow.

The shuttlecock plummeted from Robert's hand and skittered a few inches away from his feet. He stared at me for a few moments, mouth open, not comprehending. But as it sunk in, he let his neck go limp and his head dropped beneath his shoulders.

Doug smiled an evil smile.

"That's too bad," he said.

He could tell this development bothered us and enjoyed seeing us in pain.

Robert snapped his head upright. His face turned bright red, and a thick vein bulged in the center of his forehead.

"Fuck!" he said. Spit flew.

It's the only time I've ever heard him swear.

◆　　◆　　◆

I had a dream last night that they were celebrating Denzel Washington Day in Mexico. It was like watching a commercial or montage or something on TV where different people were giving brief "Happy Denzel Washington Day!" type messages in broken English, and for some reason a lot of them got confused and said Bill Washington instead of Denzel. The last one said "Bill Washington Day makes us cooler than the real Magoo!" and then I woke up.

♦ ♦ ♦

We got our clay bowls back from the kiln. Mine looks like a squished turd. Some of the glazes turn different colors once they bake, and I guess I wasn't paying much attention when I painted mine, because it's a weird swirly brownish green. Beth's bowl turned out awesome, though.

Art class is kind of an "A for Effort" kind of deal, so I still got a B+. Now we are working on construction paper mosaics.

Beth went into more detail about the crazy girls in her choir class while I cut up tiny squares of paper.

"There's a hierarchy. Molly is sort of the one calling the shots, and Tess, Bridget, and Bree are her minions. There are some other underlings who try to work their way into that upper echelon periodically."

I made a sort of "mm-hmm" sound to let her know I was listening. I never really know what to say in these types of conversations, but it seemed important to let her know that I was paying attention and what not.

Plus I was really concentrating on my paper squares. My mosaic is going to be of a dog. Dogs are like the only thing I can draw very well, so about 75% of my art is dog related, which is pretty weird 'cause we've never had a dog.

"Did you ever watch Meerkat Manor? 'Cause these girls are

exactly like the meerkats. They periodically challenge the dominant female but mostly it's like her acceptance gives them a purpose in life, so they scramble to find and secure their spot in the hierarchy. They're super mean to anyone that they feel is any kind of threat to that. They can be quite vicious about it all."

"Right."

"In a lot of ways, it's not the dominant female, Molly, who's really all that bad. The minions are the ones who get all cutthroat. And girls aren't like guys. They can't just have an aggressive confrontation and be done with it. It becomes a never-ending series of passive-aggressive insanity."

"Yeah? I don't see it, I guess. Seems like most girls are pretty nice, really."

"Oh, believe me. They know when to hide their fangs. Seriously, you would not believe the shit they're capable of."

CHAPTER 11

I CLICKED THE FLASHLIGHT ON and off again for a split second like a camera's flash. (I use the term "click" loosely here. Nick made sure to get the quietest flashlights possible.) I noted the position of the coffee table and couch corner and stayed still for a second before crawling forward the equivalent of three or four paces in the dark. I reached forward slowly, feeling along the edge of the table's glass top. It was cool enough that I could feel it through the brown cloth gloves.

I replayed our conversation from the ride over while I sat in the silent dark. Waiting.

We'd left Nick's apartment at dusk, the Malibu weaving its way through the half-light. We worked our way out toward the subdivisions we'd driven by last time. Decorative street lamps clicked on all around us.

"It's all on you tonight, man," Nick said.

"What do you mean?"

"I'll go in with you, but I'm the one waitin' by the window this time. You'll do the first sweep to see if anyone is home and what kinda loot might be up in there."

I didn't know what to say. It seemed like a terrible idea.

"Look, it ain't hard," he said. "You just move slowly and quietly and do little blasts of light with the flashlight to see where you're goin'. You make it quick as hell so nobody can see the light and be sure it was there. Man, you'd be surprised what you can get away with while people sleep. The last thing they want to believe is that someone is in their house, you know? You just have to be cautious."

He laughed.

"I'm tellin' you. I know for a fact a couple of people have seen my light before and just convinced themselves it was their imagination 'cause I turned it off so fast. And held all still and shit. They fell right back to sleep."

Another flash of light moved me into a long hallway. The light reflected off of the pale wood flooring. There were three doorways to my right and two to my left, all open. I inched down the hall. The floorboards moaned beneath me, and I stopped and held my breath.

So goddamn scared. I could hear the blood pulsing through my ears, my heart banging away. Could feel the electricity surge through the nerves and jolt my body with life. I'm talking all the way alive, too. As alive as a man can feel, anyway. Even more than the last time.

I imagine how many people go through their whole lives and never feel this, and I can't believe it. Really.

This house had been our second choice. We tried a sandy-shaded brick place first. It was all locked up. Every window and door into the place. I thought we might just head across the street or something, but Nick seemed pretty rattled. He didn't say anything. We drove a few miles away in uncomfortable silence and wound up at this white vinyl sided house with cobalt blue shutters. All the ground floor windows were locked here, too, so Nick scaled his way up onto a balcony deck. The sliding glass door slid right open.

Couldn't you just picture someone telling themselves that they wouldn't need to lock this since it's up here on the balcony?

I scuttled forward again. I shined the flashlight into the first room on the right and swung it across the room. The beam caught on a monitor, an ergonomic office chair, and a large oak desk. A pair of brown filing cabinets stood in the corner. An office. Vacant. Good.

I'd already cleared the two bedrooms (one littered with toys making it easy to identify as a kid's room, the other looked more like a hardly-ever-used guest room) and bathroom upstairs and worked my way down here. All vacant so far, aside from Nick waiting for me up by the sliding glass door.

I leaned across the hall to the first door on the left. I flipped the light on and immediately saw a light shine back at me and part of a face right next to it. I clicked the light off again within a fraction of a second and froze there. My mind raced over what all I'd taken in — white porcelain. A sink and toilet. I clicked the light back on and off again, after I realized that it'd been the bathroom mirror shining the flashlight back at me. Also vacant, of course.

I could hear the sound of a fan running in the next room on the right. I figured I knew what that meant.

The flashlight revealed a single figure lying in the fetal position in the middle of a king-sized bed, wrapped in a pink, white and blue quilt, breathing slowly and evenly. The back of the figure's head faced me, and long brown hair cascaded in all directions behind the neck and shoulders. White fabric hung down from the ceiling above in the rectangle directly over the bed. An oscillating fan in the corner provided white noise to the sleeper. And to me, too, I guess.

I squatted in the doorway for a long moment. The pitch

black nothing was all around me. It felt weird that someone was actually here. That I could hear her breathing a few feet away from me. But then I think somehow I knew the whole time that someone would be. I heard the fan about halfway down the steps, and I figured it was helping someone sleep. Maybe if it had been two people — a couple — that would've scared me. But just one... I felt in control. Like I was getting away with something.

I noticed one other detail in the bedroom as well: A jewelry box rested atop a dresser along the far wall — on the other side of the bed. I thought about going to get it. I wanted to, actually. But I thought I better leave it to Nick since he's kind of a pro or whatever.

I moved with a little more confidence now, quickly clearing a den type room with a foosball table on the left, and a storage-slash-exercise room on the right full of stacks of boxes, a recumbent bike, and a treadmill.

I crept back down the hall, felt my way in the dark along the coffee table and around the corner of the couch, and dragged myself up the steps. The sixth step creaked as I stepped on it, so I stopped and waited again. I had to keep reminding myself to keep it slow and steady.

Nick still waited by the door, motionless. I moved to him and whispered in his ear.

"There's a lady downstairs. Asleep."

It sounded weird coming out that way. I think it was the word lady that didn't sound quite right.

He whispered back.

"Anything look promisin'?"

"Saw a jewelry box in her room."

I led him down the steps to the bedroom. We kneeled outside the room while he took a quick look with his flashlight.

The woman on the bed had moved. She still lay on her side, faced away from us, but her legs were sprawled out straight now. I wanted to tell Nick, to warn him to maybe be extra quiet or something, but I couldn't.

I could sense him moving into the room somehow, though I couldn't see or hear him. All was silent for quite a while. Maybe time seems slower when you're waiting, but I've got a feeling that Nick is even more cautious than me.

Suddenly I heard a sigh and the faint sound of movement from the bed. The sound of sheet rubbing against sheet. She rolled over, and it all went quiet again. Her breathing fell back into the same slow and even pattern as before after a minute or two.

Next, I heard the slightest scraping sound, and I knew Nick must have pulled the jewelry box from the top of the dresser. No movement from the bed. No problems. I realized I was smiling like a crazy person in the dark.

After another long wait, his flailing hand tugged at my shirt when he got to the doorway. I couldn't tell if he was trying to let me know he was there or just finding his way out into the hall. We climbed the stairs, and Nick decided to look through the box as we got near the sliding glass door.

He poked through the necklaces and bracelets in the box with his left hand while his right manned the light.

"Looks like good shit," he said. "Some of it might be costume jewelry, but this is a hell of a lot more than last time, I think."

He closed the box up and tucked it under his arm. We

clambered down from the balcony and strolled off into the night like nothing happened.

♦   ♦   ♦

Nick was giddy on the ride home. (Maybe I was, too.) His pupils were all dilated. His knuckles turned white 'cause he was gripping the steering wheel so hard.

The night stretched out around us as far as we could see and farther. Infinite.

We drove aimlessly through suburbs and rural patches. Fresh air gushed in at us through the four open windows, and when we got going fast enough, there was a weird pulsing sound like a helicopter from something to do with the air flow and open windows. Nick fixed it by putting right front and left rear windows most of the way up. I didn't really understand it, but the helicopter noise stopped, so who cares?

"I know you get it now," he said. "I can see it."

"Yeah?"

He nodded.

"You're stronger than you was. The way you handle yourself and everythin'. You're not scared. Not like you was."

I didn't know what to say, so I just said:

"Yeah."

"Maybe you can't see it yet, but you've changed. I can tell you've got a lot of grit to you now. I always figured you did, but you might have more than I thought even."

He smiled at me. He actually seemed proud, which kind of weirded me out.

♦   ♦   ♦

As the car ride continued, the giddiness faded to a dull glow. The road gashed a strip of pavement through dark woods. Vines hung down from most of the branches. We wandered again.

"Somethin' I've been meanin' to tell you," Nick said.

"Yeah?"

"Already told you about avoidin' houses with dogs. But if you're in one of these houses, and you come upon a dog, and that dog starts barkin' which they usually do, you gotta strangle it."

I held my breath for a second.

"What?"

"You've got to. It might be, like, a life or death choice. If the dog gets the attention of the owner, they could shotgun blast you in the face or call the cops and get you locked up."

He shook his head before continuing.

"Gotta kill it."

I was quiet for a moment. The headlights caught on swarms of bugs hovering above the road.

"I don't know if I can do that," I said.

"Look, you eat meat, don't you?"

"Well, yeah."

"Well, they slaughter 400 cattle per hour in those meat plants. I read a book about it. It's like a concentration camp. So you're part of killin' animals every day of your life or close to it. Killin' one dog ain't nothin' compared to that. Nothin'."

He felt his pocket and pulled out a cigarette pack, but it was empty. He crushed it and tossed it to the floor.

"We all eat meat. We all kill. I'm just honest about it. I

grasp the reality of it and deal with it. Everyone else — all the limp dick yuppies and shit — they lie to themselves. They only see slices of red stuff in styrofoam at the supermarket like it was grown in a lab somewhere. I see the blood and death. How many of them do you really think would slit a cow's throat themselves for a meal? Not so many, right? But they're still part of it. They still support it in droves. The end result is the same as if they did it."

I wanted to say something, but I couldn't think. He pushed his knees up to hold the steering wheel steady and pantomimed a strangling motion, his hands choking the air between us.

"You gotta get 'em high on the throat. Right under the chin. Push in with your thumbs to close the wind pipe, and then just squeeze like a motherfucker."

CHAPTER 12

I WENT TO BETH'S TODAY after school. It was weird. We ate quiche with her parents, who asked me a bunch of inane questions like where I lived and what my parents did for a living and such. After that we had this crappy cheap Neapolitan ice cream, and Beth's mom did this weird thing.

"Are you sure you want to be eating all of that?" she said, raising her eyebrows at Beth.

Beth stopped eating and just looked down. And she threw the rest of her ice cream away after that. It sucked. I wanted to throw mine away, but I had to be polite and finish it. It tasted like fake bullshit.

She didn't really seem like she was in the mood to hang out after that, so I took off before long. It was still interesting to actually spend some time at her house, though. It was nothing like where I live. I am officially a working-class guy aspiring for the hand of an upper-middle-class girl. They had vaulted ceilings and a wide variety of decorative plants. They could photograph this shit and put it in some kind of Martha Stewart magazine or something.

If they ever make a magazine called "Modest Living," I think our apartment could be in there, though.

♦　♦　♦

Got my payment from Nick today. $765. That is like so much

money!

Turns out crime totally pays.

It's weird 'cause I've never really understood the appeal of jewelry in the first place. People seem to get off on the monetary value of the precious metals and jewels more than they actually like them. They repeat little marketing bullshit slogans like "princess cut diamonds" and stuff. Total nonsense. Nothing makes me want to vomit more than the diamond commercials at Christmas, too.

I don't know. I leave luxury for the rich. I guess I don't leave it, actually. I steal luxury from the rich and pawn it for spending money. I'm like a selfish modern-day Robin Hood, really.

♦ ♦ ♦

In Psychology today we talked about how there's this theory that it takes 10,000 hours to become an expert at something. So if I started playing drums today, let's say, it'd take me 10,000 hours of practice to become an expert level drummer. That means if I put in a good three hours a day of practice, it'd take a little over nine years. It's crazy that you can boil it down to that.

A series of simple steps. Practice. Repeat.

It's all just wiring it in your brain, though. Experience and repetition are the biggest things. Every day is a chance to get better and better and better at whatever you want to do. Or whoever you want to be, I guess.

♦ ♦ ♦

So maybe I have changed after all.

I was standing by my locker after lunch. Just standing. Thinking. Staring off into space. I was half watching this weird freshman kid who wears cut up socks as wrist bands drag his hand along the lockers as he walked way down the hall.

Eventually, I turned around and looked up to see Troy. He walked right up to me, scowling. I mean, right up in my face. But I didn't look away. I didn't break eye contact or take a step back. I didn't even wait for him to speak. I just stood up a little straighter and looked down at him. And I said:

"You better back the fuck up."

The hallway was empty aside from us. I could feel my lip curl up over my teeth like a growling dog's.

"Yeah?" he said. "Or what?"

"Or I'll be pissin' in your mouth after I knock you out."

(Kinda stole it from Nick. So yeah.)

His head twitched, and his eyes looked off to the side. He looked confused. And like he was totally going to back down. I probably could've left it at that.

But instead I grabbed him by the shoulders and tossed him to the ground like a rag doll. It was like nothing. He landed on his back, slapping against the terrazzo floor and half-rolling like an upside down turtle. And without thinking I stomped on the ankle that I thought was the bad one. My heel bashed at him with all of my weight behind it. He moaned like a girl and pulled his legs up against his chest to protect his limbs, curled up in a little ball.

I felt crazy. Like my brain was on fire. But I kind of liked it.

Just then, the Physics teacher Mr. Row poked his head out of his classroom, saw Troy crumpled on the ground and said:

103

"What's going on out here?"

I laughed.

"We were just messing around," I said and smiled at Troy.

He didn't say a goddamn word and didn't make eye contact with me. He picked himself up and limped away.

So you might be reading this and thinking that it was a mistake. That I just opened a big can o' wormies, and this guy is going to get me back. That he won't just let this go.

And the truth is that I don't give a fuck. Fuck him. And looking at him on the ground, I know that he knows that I don't give a fuck. And he's not going to do a goddamn thing unless he wants his teeth knocked down his goddamn throat.

◆　◆　◆

Sheesh. Pretty aggressive last time. Sorry about that, dude.

Even now when I think about it, though, I get mad. It's the weirdest thing. I mean, is that normal? Is this what other people have been feeling all of this time, and I've just been disconnected from it or something? (Until now, I mean.)

In any case, I am not scared now. That is the truth. I don't want to say that I feel powerful, 'cause that sounds weird, but I feel in control of myself. Like before I didn't know how to protect myself and now I somehow do. I thought I would need to learn like fighting techniques or something, but it's not like that. It's like some animal thing just clicked into place, and everything makes sense now or something.

I wonder if it's a right brain thing. Like somewhere in our right brain there is this primal instinct to survive and protect yourself, and we're all coded to know how to do that. But before it was locked away from me somehow, and now it's not.

I don't know. Don't worry too much about it, though. This episode aside, I plan to only use my powers for good.

CHAPTER 13

WE HUNG OUT AT BETH'S for a little while after school today. Her parents weren't home, so it was just us.

Her mom has a huge aquarium full of tropical fish. I mean, ginormous. The only other places I've ever seen aquariums that big are restaurants and dentist offices. Or does not everyone's dentist office have a big ass fish tank? I don't know.

Anyway, I was looking at the fish, and Beth came over and handed me a can of Diet Coke. I guess she doesn't know that guys don't drink Diet Coke. Maybe, like, older fat men do, but that's about it, I think.

"Ridiculous, huh?" she said.

"What is?"

"The fish. They're like the least interesting, least practical pet ever. You can have absolutely no interaction with them. They're just there to look at and be pretty. It's like buying a pair of shoes that swims around in a tank. It takes more effort to grow flowers than it does to have this stupid fish tank."

She slurped from the can.

"I guess I never thought about it before," I said.

"Maybe some people with fish actually kind of care about them, though I don't really see how. My mom doesn't, though. They die all the time, and she just replaces them with new ones."

I watched a bright blue fish wriggle through a patch of fake seaweed.

"That one," Beth pointed to a big ugly purplish brown fish with huge lips. "He eats the other fish. And not like he just swallows it whole. He takes little bites out of them slowly over time, until they die."

"Jesus," I said.

"Yeah."

♦   ♦   ♦

Another epiphany in Mrs. Francis' class today. Unreal. She was talking about the biosphere and hydrosphere and related crap about various 'spheres. Not that I really heard much of it.

I should set the scene with this little nugget, though: the radiator in that classroom is insane. On even a remotely crisp fall today, such as today, the thing kicks into overdrive. Kicks out heat non-stop until it feels like it's about 80 degrees in there. A dry heat that almost seems to hug you. Somehow not uncomfortable.

In any case, I think that extra warmth in the air casts this sleepy pall over the room. Flushes the cheeks. Makes the eyelids grow heavy.

But let's not be hasty and give the radiator all the credit here. The soothing tones of Marsha Francis have knocked unconscious many an otherwise strong, vibrant youth. Flipped their power switch. Put their lights out. Myself included. I don't think I was truly asleep today, but damn near.

Dude, I don't know what it is about that nasal voice of hers, but within about ninety seconds of 'sphere talk, my mind had fled the confines of the biology lab and crept out into the astral plane or something. For real, my thoughts were so clear, and so strong, it was like a dream. I sort of forgot where I was and all that.

Whilst out there in the dream world, I managed to download some sweet wisdom into my noggin, too. Bonus lesson — no Nick required.

Here's what I realized:

When you're a kid, life mostly happens to you. You have no control. No say.

But then you get older, and at some point, you start making things happen. Start choosing things. What you do. Where you go. And smaller things like what you wear and your haircut and all that.

Whatever you want. Whatever you need. You choose it all.

Your life belongs to you. Finally.

If you do things right, it's like you can finally begin making the world happen around you instead of the world making you happen. You can participate instead of observe.

You can venture into new worlds, like I did by going along with Nick. You can change. Upgrade yourself. Transform into someone of your own making.

Or you can coast. Stay inside the lines society and your parents drew around you. Let the world keep on deciding who you are, where you go, what you want. Stay on that beaten path everyone is always talking about.

So that's kind of your choice in life as you reach adulthood, I think. Do you change, or do you coast? Do you choose the path of your life, or do you let it happen to you?

It's not as simple as it seems at first. Changing creates a risk, right? Heading outside those lines, braving your way into a new world? It's a leap of faith. Leaves you vulnerable and in some ways alone.

'Cause maybe it won't work. Maybe you'll fail. Get hurt. Embarrass yourself.

Or maybe it's an effort. Hard work. Uncomfortable. Maybe you have to take your lumps before you get this new world figured out. Maybe the price you pay to change will be too big.

Plus, you have to actually do something, which no one wants, believe me.

Coasting, though? Coasting is easy. It feels pretty good, I imagine, to just give in. Go with the flow. Let the whims of the world pull you along through the days. No real worries. No real cares at all.

But you know what? I've done my share of coasting in my fifteen years. Not good. Coasting makes you sick at heart, that's what I think. It traps you inside those lines, inside whatever box the world has put you in. It constricts around you like some big ass snake. Holds you still. Never lets you grow. Never lets you fuckin' breathe.

It's stasis, and stasis is death, I say.

So that changes the choice, doesn't it?

Changing or coasting is not the choice you're making here. It's *do or die.*

Me? I reached a point of despair, I guess. Coasted too long. Got picked on. And before all this stuff with Nick — the lessons and everything, I mean — I felt so small. Felt sick, like I said. Sick somewhere in my soul.

Weak and worthless. A nothing. A nobody.

I couldn't let it stay that way. I couldn't sit on my hands any longer. I had to *do*. Something. Anything. Had to.

And I did. Crazy as it seems to me even still, I did.

Like when I stop and think about everything that has happened, it kind of blows my mind. With Nick. With Beth. With Troy. I made all of that happen. I chose my path, and I got after it, and I made this little piece of the world mine.

No one handed me these things. They happened because I willed them, enacted them, grabbed hold of them.

And it's an incredible feeling. I write the story of my life now. No one else. I dare to live it the way I want.

Do or die.

Everything comes down to that. In life. In love. In the universe.

Do or die.

♦　♦　♦

I took Beth to Nick's today. Not intentionally. I mean, I'm not an idiot.

It started as a walk and talk. A stroll. I thought I was walking Beth home, as a matter of fact. Eventually I realized that we were kind of meandering some other direction, no destination from what I could tell.

I stopped in my tracks, toes just shy of a huge crack in the sidewalk. Looking back, I see that I should have stayed in-G mode, should have played it cool. Maybe I could have steered things a different way. Why not just go with the flow or whatever? Enjoy the walk.

"Wait. Where are we going?" I said.

"Nowhere," she said. "Why, you have to be somewhere or something?"

"No. I just…"

I considered telling her that I thought I was walking her home, but I could no longer see a point in it.

"I have to go to the bathroom, actually," she said.

I thought about the nearest available shitter.

"Broad Street is only a couple blocks that way."

I pointed in the direction of everyone's favorite liquor store.

Beth's face scrunched up, the wrinkles on her nose reading as either disgusted or vicious.

"What?" I said.

"Isn't that…. I mean, wouldn't the bathroom there be… you know…"

"Disgusting beyond words?" I said, offering an end to her sentence.

"Yeah."

"I mean, pretty much."

A montage of the atrocities I'd witnessed in the unisex bathroom at the liquor store flashed through my head. All manner of bodily fluids spattered over the toilet seat and tank, piled (or pooled) on the floor, smeared on the subway tiled walls hung up around the throne. Let's just say fifty shades of brown, varying levels of solidity.

"Well, my cousin lives right up here. Almost as close as the store."

Regret stabbed me repeatedly in the belly and face as soon as the words were out. Brutal. Violent thrusts of bitterness. What was I thinking?

Relief showed on Beth's face right away, though. I can see how anything would have sounded better than the alternative.

We walked on. Beth talked, but I had a hard time focusing on her words. I could only picture Nick and Donnie with psychotic smiles on their faces upon our arrival.

My heart kicked up into a gallop as we climbed the steps and crossed the porch. I realized that my hand was shaking a little as I reached out to turn the doorknob, but I don't think Beth saw.

Inside, however, we found neither Nick nor Donnie. Instead Tammie sat half-sprawled on the couch, a mass market paperback in her hands. I think it was a Dean Koontz book.

She did smile upon seeing the two of us, but it wasn't psychotic. More like sisterly, I'd say. Tammie is nice.

I introduced the two of them, and then Beth scurried off to the bathroom. Honestly, if I had to guess, it was a number two. Just a hunch.

"Nick's not here?" I said, taking a seat on the couch.

Tammie shook her head.

"He and Donnie got a tip on a bunch of scrap metal left on the side of the road. Some building demo or something, I guess. They're borrowing Roy Nygaard's truck to try to haul it and sell it."

That did sound exactly like something they'd do. So I'd lucked out. Missed them. I didn't really know why I wanted to shield Beth from them. I only knew that I really, really did.

When Beth reentered the room, Tammie stood, and that little smile crept back over her mouth.

"Either of you want some yerba mate?"

"What's that?" I said.

"Well, it's tea. But it's not normal tea. It has… medicinal properties, I guess you could say."

"Like what?" Beth said.

"Well, it gives you energy, but it's not like caffeine, though it has a little of that in it as well. I'd say there's something simultaneously invigorating and calming about it. Mildly euphoric. It's really popular in South America, I think. I bet you guys would like it. I mean, I think it's awesome."

"I'll try some," I said.

"Me too," Beth said.

Tammie disappeared into the kitchen and returned a few minutes later with steaming mugs of yerba mate.

"I added a splash of milk. I hope that's OK. That's how I like it."

Beth and I murmured agreeable sounds and took our mugs from her.

I stared down into the pale fluid. Felt the heat coil off of it to brush its wet at my chin.

I took a drink. It tingled all the way down. Something a little magical about it. It could have just been the sheer heat, I suppose, but I don't think so. Something more. The taste was good, too. Like a spicy chai, I think.

I exchanged a glance with Beth, and we both kind of nodded. She liked it, too.

About halfway through the mug, the little rush hit me. Nothing too intense. But it was just like Tammie said. I felt incredibly energetic yet calm. Very, very pleasant. Much more enjoyable than the coffee jitters, I'd say.

"This is awesome," Beth said.

I nodded with gusto.

"Yeah? I thought you'd like it," Tammie said. "Nick doesn't like it. I don't know how that can be, but he doesn't. Says it makes him feel like not himself or something like that."

"Well, he's wrong," I said. "It's fucking great."

That got a little laugh out of them, and I noticed that both of these girls — the two women I am closest to in the world, I realize — were just glowing. I don't mean so much in the sense of physical beauty as I do that they beamed happiness like it was a light shining out of their faces. Real, pure, unapologetic joy.

We fell quiet after that, though it was a comfortable silence. All sipping our tea. Feeling good. Smiling at each other.

And I felt so together with these two girls. Close to them. In sync with them in this simple moment of human closeness.

And I think maybe these are the most important times in life and also the most fleeting. Those moments of pure companionship. Nothing complicated. Nothing heated. The little slices of time when you want for nothing, when you simply enjoy the company of people you care about, people you connect with, with or without words.

You stop thinking for a little bit and simply be.

Connection. Closeness.

They are vexing in the way they elude us, slip away from us, but when you find them, it is wonderful, even if it's only for a little while.

"How'd you find out about this?" I said, breaking the little spell. "The yerba mate, I mean."

Tammie took a sip before she answered.

"Heard about it on the Joe Rogan Experience."

"You're into Joe Rogan?" Beth said, a little laugh coming out with her words.

Tammie shrugged, smiled again.

"Nick likes it, so I end up hearing quite a bit."

Somehow we all ended up chuckling a little at this, that

glow once more touching both of their faces.

And then I looked up and realized Nick stood in the doorway to the living room.

It startled me pretty good. I don't know why, but it did. That joy seeped right out of me, deflated like it was a tire that'd run over a nail.

I stood up right away, almost spilled my last swallow of tea. "Oh, hey, Nick," I said.

He didn't say anything. Didn't even really look at me so much as gaze around the room, eyes all dark and shifting and impossible to read.

After a long beat, he turned and walked away. Not a word.

"What's his problem?" I said to Tammie, keeping my voice quiet.

"See, I was hoping you might know. I think you're the only one who could maybe figure him out one of these days."

Beth and I didn't stay long after that, though we didn't discuss leaving. We just kind of spontaneously gathered our things and got out.

Thinking back on it now, it was the only time I've ever felt unwelcome at Nick's.

CHAPTER 14

NICK HELD UP ONE SIDE of the garage door about a foot off the ground, and I snaked under it on my belly. For some reason the latch on this side was just loose enough that you could pry the door a hair open like that. I had no idea why Nick thought to try it, but he did, and now I was in.

I waited in the dark to let things go all quiet. I figured, this being the garage, I didn't need to be quite as cautious, so it was only about a minute before I shined my flashlight for a second and swept it around the room. Empty. Not just void of human life. Void of just about everything except for a vinyl tarp crumpled in the back corner. Cracks gashed the length of the concrete floor, so I made sure not to trip as I moved through the blackness to unlock the deadbolt on the entry door and let Nick in.

He checked the room with his light as well, and we moved through another door into the house to inspect its contents. Nick flashed his light again, and swung it past a dishwasher, sink, cabinets and empty spots cut into the counter where a stove and fridge should be. Again, the room was completely empty aside from the clusters of dust hugging along the edges of everything. He sighed loudly.

"Well, we done it this time," he whispered. "We busted into an abandoned property."

He stood and moved quickly down the hallway, not bothering to conceal the sound of his footsteps. He wiggled his light into a few more rooms.

"Fuck!"

He yelled, which startled me. I mean, it made sense that the house was empty, but I needed more time than that to adjust out of silent mode.

"So it's abandoned?" I said, still squatting and whispering.

"It's a foreclosure, most likely. Usually we can avoid 'em because of the for sale signs, but there are so many foreclosed homes right now that a lot of them aren't even for sale. There are just tons of empty houses settin' out there. Just rottin' away."

I stood up and brushed some of the dirt off from crawling under the garage door.

"So do we go on to the next one?" I said.

He shook his head.

"My only rule is one house per night. Once you enter one home, you're done, whether you find anything or not. We might as well check it all out, though. Just in case."

The upstairs was empty aside from a couple cans of Smurf blue paint in one of the bedroom closets. It was a weird place. Ornate designs covered the carpet throughout in a really classless way, like a Vegas casino had vomited everywhere. The basement door had a clasp for a padlock on it, which Nick undid so we could take the steps down.

"Why would you need to lock the basement from this side?" I said.

"Who knows?" he said.

We passed through the door, and I noticed that the other side also had a padlock clasp, so you could lock it from either side. Weird. As we ventured out into the open concrete of the basement floor, Nick started laughing. He shined his light along the ceiling. I had no idea what was so funny.

"Someone has already cleaned this place out," he said. "See that? The plumbin' is all ripped out. Most of it, anyway. The copper pipes. Someone sold 'em for scrap."

He sighed again and slapped the glass block basement window over his shoulder like he was giving it a high five.

"We picked a real winner tonight, Jake."

We filed back up the stairs and milled around in the kitchen for a minute. Nick seemed to be trying to calm himself down.

"Eh... It happens," he said. "You can't win 'em all. And it always could've been much, much worse."

"Why'd you think to try the garage door like that, anyway?" I said.

"I could see that it was bent, and there were black marks, too, like someone had slammed into it. The lockin' mechanisms on older doors like these use these long flat bars that get bent really easily. I figured if someone hit this door with a car hard enough to dent it like that, one side or the other might be a little wonky."

My plan worked. We walked out as he explained it all, and I left the garage door unlocked. He was too distracted explaining himself to notice. I was thinking I might bring Beth back to this empty house at some point. I didn't know whether or not Nick would care, but my instinct was to hide it from him, so I did.

◆　◆　◆

School was only a half day today for some kind of teacher

in-service thing. Half days are always weird. All the kids just roam around town all afternoon like nomads. Looking for action.

I didn't really feel like going home, you know, so I kind of followed along with this group of kids. They were all these computer nerd types that play role-playing games and stuff. I know a couple of them from my food science class. Trevor and David.

We kind of meandered for a while until someone mentioned food.

"Let's go to 7-11," David said. So we did.

I grabbed some Little Debbies and Funyuns. I think seeing that guy in my Psychology class eating them all the time made me want to get them. Having had them again, I can confirm that they are not great.

Trevor bought not one, but two flavors of Doritos and one of those shitty little apple pies.

"This is my secret recipe," Trevor explained. "You gotta crunch up the Cool Ranch Doritos and then pour them into the bag of Nacho Cheese Doritos. Like a seasoning."

"And the pie?" I asked.

"Huh?"

"Does the apple pie figure into the recipe?"

"Oh no. The pie is more of a palate cleanser," he said.

David also got Doritos. They seemed to be really into Doritos, actually, now that I look back on it.

Anyway, we just roved around downtown eating this terrible food. Gorging ourselves with sugar and saturated fat.

This other kid got this like cheeseburger hot dog. It's like a burger dog with gooey American cheese inside of it that sits in the damn rotisserie for who knows how long. 89 cents. He slathered it up with a bunch of Miracle Whip, too. Like three packets. Unbelievable.

We wandered a long time. Walked down these train tracks for quite a ways and wound up behind this sewage treatment plant with a humongous swirling tank of, I believe, turds. There's this giant metal arm stirring this big open tank of brown sludge. Gurgling. Churning. I assume it's human shit, but I guess it seems pretty weird, right? It was all fenced up, so we observed it from afar.

"You guys think any of that poop is ours?" This kid, Aaron, asked.

"I hope not," Trevor said. "I don't like to think about my turds mixing with a bunch of Stranger Turds."

We crossed this wooden bridge and wove our way through a graveyard along the edge of the woods. There was an oversized headstone for a guy named Benjamin Blood that served as a decent conversation piece. Yeah, yeah. The Curious Case of Benjamin Blood and all that.

Eventually I kind of splintered off from the group and headed home. When I got to my apartment, Beth was sitting outside on the astroturf swathed front steps, her face all puffed and red. Her pale blue eyes fastened on mine for a second and then flicked to the ground. She looked so sad.

"Can I come in?" she said.

This was not how I envisioned Beth's first trip to my house going. We sat on the edge of my bed and didn't say much. She cried some. I tried to ask her what was wrong, but she didn't want to talk about it.

"I will tell you," she said. "I promise I will. But not today."

Thinking back now, I guess I was pretty caught up in the drama of it all 'cause I didn't even get embarrassed of my dumb room or how crappy my house is compared to hers and all of that.

I mean, Jesus. It's not much of a bedroom. The frayed bedspread with sky blue and pink boxes on it. (Thanks, Mom!) The red carpet that looks like it belongs in a 1986 funeral home. The weird scratches and grooves along one wall that look like an animal desperately tried to claw through it at some point. The brown water stains on the ceiling. The sulfur smell wafting in from the bathroom.

Yep. Those are just some of the features that made our apartment a must-rent.

Beth scooted up onto the edge of the bed and rotated her shoulders toward me a little bit.

"Thank you," she said.

"For what?"

"For always being here for me."

She brushed her hair out of her eyes and went on.

"Even when I'm a mess like this. Or especially when I am, I guess. You're always there when I need you."

"Oh..." I said. "Well, you're welcome, you know."

She leaned forward and kissed me. Just a peck on the lips. I didn't know what to say, so I didn't say anything. Or move. Or breathe. I think I almost went into convulsions.

She leaned back and laughed. Maybe I looked funny or something. The look in her eye kind of changed all of a sudden. She leaned in and kissed me again, but this was not a peck. It was aggressive. Her mouth dropped open as she approached in a way that reminded me of a fish.

Warm. Tongue action. Moisture.

Not really sure how to say this. I mean, it was awesome, you know. I felt good. And I was kind of in disbelief that it was really happening. But all I could think about was that I was going to need to towel off the lower half of my face after this. She was getting all juicy and drooling all down my chin and stuff. Seriously. I don't want to complain, but... Entirely too much saliva.

Maybe there's something not ladylike about the whole thing, which I know is an odd thing to say. Seriously like a weird, old-fashioned thing to say, but I already said it, so...

She seemed happy enough after that, so I was glad and all. I mean, I was still excited and everything. I don't know.

Maybe sometimes when you want something for long enough, once you have it, it can't even seem real somehow. Does that make sense? Maybe. Maybe not.

We watched Dr. Phil after that. He told some parents who spoil their teenage daughters to "get real."

CHAPTER 15

ANOTHER NIGHT. ANOTHER HOUSE. IT was a big Tudor place in a cluster of rich-looking houses nestled among an otherwise shitty neighborhood. In fact, it was the big steel fence and gate surrounding the home that initially piqued our interest.

I crawled through the dark on all fours, hands and feet bobbing and scrabbling. I clamped my flashlight between my teeth like a pirate's blade.

The bursts of light brought me pictures of wall-to-wall yellow shag carpet and those shitty tan couches with prints of like a stream and a water wheel at a mill or something on them. Hideous. The TV looked like one of those huge wooden ones from the late 70s or early 80s. The décor did not exactly convey any promise of concealed riches, but I supposed you never know for sure.

I wouldn't say I moved more quickly than before, really, but now I moved with more confidence somehow. I felt no real fear, I think. Just excitement and anticipation and all of that. I'd put in some reps. My brain was wired to do this now.

I shuffled down the final hallway, swinging my lamp about like a lightsaber. All the rooms came up empty. We'd wound up at another place with no one home somehow. That foreclosure aside, Nick seemed to have a knack for picking houses.

I double-checked the bedroom — still empty, obviously —

and circled back to the back door where Nick was waiting. (We'd spent about twenty minutes peeling off screens only to find locked windows. Then Nick tried the rear door. Unlocked. I think it wasn't even closed all the way.) Now the real search began in earnest as we picked through the heaps of junk looking for valuables.

We started in the bedroom, Nick dumping the dresser drawers and the few wooden boxes on the dresser top. He sifted, paused to look over an item and went back to sifting. Nothing of interest.

After a look under the bed revealed only cobwebs, I slid open the drawer in the bedside table. A string of beads rested in there that, for a split second, I thought were large pearls. Next to that were two more balls, metal this time, on a string. My hand moved to them but stopped short. Something made me hesitate.

"What are these?" I said.

Nick leaned over to peer into the drawer. He laughed.

"Those are ben wa balls."

"Oh," I said. "What's that?"

He laughed again. He pointed to the metal balls.

"Well... you stick those in the girl's cooter."

("Cooter." People actually say that, and some of them are even related to me. Unbelievable.)

"And then there on the right you got some anal beads," he said. "I think you know where those go."

Yikes. We didn't speak for a moment.

"What the hell is wrong with people?" I said.

Nick shrugged.

♦ ♦ ♦

Further tearing through the house failed to reward us, though we didn't find any more creepy sex toys, at least. We dug through the kitchen a second time. Nick grew more and more agitated. He didn't say anything, but I could read it in the deepening folds and creases on his face.

I got the sense that we were about to give up on this one — the gated English Tudor full of thrift store furniture, I mean — and Nick's slumped shoulders seemed to confirm that notion. For whatever reason, though, we decided to check the garage.

It was one of those garages cluttered with junk, but I still saw it as soon as he opened the door. The street light angling through the window made a rectangle of light that stretched across the garage. It provided just enough illumination for me to make out the silhouette of the dial and handle protruding from the box-shaped item overhead. Balanced on a stack of boards laid across the exposed beams above us was a small safe.

"A safe in the garage?" I said. "Up in the rafters?"

Nick grimaced.

"What?"

I had just assumed that he'd seen it, too, and it felt a little weird that he'd failed to. The pupil had outdone the master for once. I pointed to the safe. His jaw dropped, and he wiped at his lips with the back of his hand.

"Good fuckin' eye," he said and clapped me on the shoulder.

We circled under the safe like sharks closing in on a surfer with a scraped knee.

Nick's body language changed entirely. His chest swelled, and his posture righted itself. He took long strides, pacing back

125

and forth, eyes glued to the safe.

"The only question now," he said, "is how we gonna get the goddamn thing down?"

It was a fair question. The safe was about ten-to-twelve feet up, and there was no ladder in the garage. The only thing tall enough to stand on and reach it was the top of a workbench nowhere near close enough to be of any help.

"Get on my shoulders," I said.

"Are you sure?"

"Yep."

"I'm gonna have to actually stand on your shoulders to able to reach."

"I know."

I stooped, and he stepped the first foot onto my shoulder.

"This is like some cheerleader shit right here," he said.

He jammed the heel of his hand into the top of my head, presumably for balance, and swung his other foot up. His feet straddled my neck, digging into those muscles between the neck and shoulder. You know how kids jam their fingers there in gym class to hit some pressure point and fuck each other up? It felt like that, basically. And then when he stood up, it felt like a horse digging his two stupid hooves into those muscles. I made some kind of grunting noise.

"You alright?" he said.

"Yeah."

I clasped my hands around his ankles and prepared myself for the physical exertion of rising with a human being standing on me. My legs locked up as I stood, like my knees just wouldn't uncoil for a second, but I pushed a little harder and got through it. He wobbled a little and grabbed one of the beams to catch himself.

"Alright," he said. "Take one pace forward."

I obliged. He put his hands on the safe and sort of patted around the bottom and sides as he considered how to proceed.

"Little closer," he said.

I shuffled forward a bit. He leaned a little, his feet grinding that much further into my shoulders, and hugged around the safe. It was high enough that he was kind of just hugging it to his face more than anything. The embrace only lasted a few seconds. He pulled back, repositioned himself and hugged it again.

"Damn," he said. "Ain't got no leverage."

Again, he released the safe and leaned back on the beam. He paused a moment, mopping at his mouth again with the back of his hand.

"So what are we gonna do?" I said. "'Cause if you could make it snappy... That'd be tremendous."

"I'm thinking. Believe it or not, I don't want to drop the fuckin' thing on your foot," he said.

I pictured my foot smashed flat like in a cartoon. Then I pictured it again but this time it just exploded into a bloody spray.

"Well, I can respect that," I said.

"You'd drop me," he said.

For a second I'd actually believed he'd been concerned with the welfare of my feet.

"We'll get it," he said. "This is like the ultimate. I fuckin' love safes. Ain't no way we're leavin' this thing behind."

He tapped a hand on the beam as he thought.

"Wait," he said.

"Waiting," I said.

He leaned forward again, and by now it felt like he was wearing golf spikes. I was certain that my shoulders were bleeding.

He fumbled at the boards holding the safe up, his fingers crawling along the edges and latching around each side of one corner. He strained to lift, and the board rose an inch. The safe didn't budge. He let go and the board slammed back down.

"OK, this will work," he said. "Take three paces forward."

He ducked down as I moved under the board.

"Just keep a hold of my ankles, alright?" he said.

"OK."

"I gotta do a fuckin' military press type deal," he said. "And I might lose my balance a little."

He popped up, carrying some of the momentum of the drive of his legs into the board as his hands connected with it and drove one side straight up. The safe slid off the tilted surface and crashed to the floor a few feet away from us. It was loud as hell, but it landed safely. (Pun intended.)

I'm proud to confirm that no feet were harmed during this production. Actually, the crazy thing was that the safe also took no damage at all.

I kneeled and Nick climbed down from my shoulders. Suddenly that cliché about the weight of the world lifting from your shoulders made a lot more sense. I felt so light. I brushed some of the grit away from where his feet had been.

Nick stood over the fallen safe, beaming.

"No damage! This thing is like a got-damn tank!" he said.

◆　◆　◆

We lugged the safe out the back door of the garage and walked around the house. It was heavy, and more than that, it was awkward. The top of the safe leaned into Nick's chest where he hugged around it, and I kind of squat-walked behind it holding up the bottom. Between his walking backward and my crouch and stumble, it was really goddamn slow going.

I heard a rumble as we turned the corner from the back to the side of the garage, but I didn't think much of it. It didn't seem all that loud compared to the sound of Nick and I crunching through the dry sticks of some dead plant life underfoot. Nick showed no signs of noticing it either.

Instead his face contorted all crazily, and veins protruded from his neck and forehead like he had a couple of thick orange extension cords running through those areas. Something about his teeth looked very rodent-like in this state.

As we rounded the corner toward the front of the house, we passed through a narrow opening between a bush and a pine tree. Nick stopped in that tiny gap, and I ran my thighs into the corner of the safe, which hurt. I was about to ask him what the hell when I suddenly noticed that the rumbling was much louder.

I glanced over to see a running car in the driveway only a few yards away from us. The headlights were off. A light-colored Toyota Corolla. White, I think. Maybe silver.

It was too dark to tell if someone was actually in the car, but when the rumble died, I knew someone must have turned off the ignition. The engine made a few little "tink" metallic sounds as it wound down, and then it fell silent completely. I could hear the muffled jingle of the keys inside, and then the click of the door opening.

The dome light revealed an older couple. A fat bald man with a white beard, and a woman with long gray hair. I immediately pictured the drawer with the ben wa balls and shuddered inside.

They climbed out of the vehicle, the old man stretching a moment before they moved toward the house.

"We forgot to stop for milk," the old woman said.

"We'll get 'er tomorrow," the old man said.

"Alright, but that means black coffee in the morning."

"That's fine."

I realized, belatedly, that they hadn't seen us at all. It seemed too ridiculous. That we could just freeze here like a couple of fucking groundhogs or something and get away with this. Nothing to see here. No, no. Just two statues clutching a safe. They veered away from us, heading up the walk toward the front door.

As soon as they crossed the threshold into the house, we took off, racing to the car and tossing the safe into the backseat before speeding off into the night. Nick couldn't stop laughing the whole time.

CHAPTER 16

WHEN I WAS A KID, one of the Little League teams was named after a local supermarket called Miller's. So the kids on the other teams would chant:

"Miller's, Miller's, butthole fillers!"

Isn't that, like, insanely graphic for a bunch of eight-year-olds? You would hear this up and down the streets at all hours.

CHAPTER 17

IN PSYCHOLOGY TODAY WE TALKED about how different cultures have a different sense of "self." So for example, in the United States we believe strongly in our individuality, independence, and self-esteem. We have a sense of our self being a concrete thing. I guess that's why a lot of (not all) people here are so comfortable labeling themselves and aspiring to fit that label. Punk kids dress a certain way and value a certain set of things. Preppie kids (even if they wouldn't call themselves that) would be embarrassed to wear non-name brand stuff that doesn't reflect the class and social group they identify with. And so on.

In Eastern cultures, they have a much looser sense of all of this. They see the needs of the community and family as more important than things like independence and individuality. They see themselves not as a concrete self, but merely a collection of thoughts, values, and preferences. Something that shifts and changes over time. They don't make decisions through a weird identity filter as much as we do. They don't pick a certain brand of cola because of what it might say about them. They aren't perpetually self-conscious and stroking their own ego with every goddamn thing they do.

They're just here. And they're experiencing life. That's all.

Here it's like everything is weird egotistical consumption, you know? I buy this brand of shoes because that's who I am. I watch this TV show because that's who I am. I have the newest

Iphone/Ipad whatever gadget because that's who I am. And it's insane because there is nothing emptier than consumption.

Like the goddamn idiots that line up around the block to get whatever new Apple gadget. They have this fervor about them like it's a religious experience. Like they want it to be that. Desperately. They want to be so excited about this gadget, because maybe this time it will give their life meaning. But it doesn't. It just means you can watch episodes of Top Chef on a small tablet instead of on TV.

So congratulations.

◆　◆　◆

First image at Nick's today: Donnie pressing a stethoscope to the safe as he twisted the dial around all slow. Hilarious. He had this little toolkit out, like all of a sudden he's a safecracker in an old western movie or something.

"Almost got it," Donnie said. It was about the eighth time he'd said that.

"I'm telling you guys. The way to crack this safe is a little thing I like to call brute force. Just sledgehammer that shit," I said.

Nick seemed to be buying into Donnie's act.

"Nah, man. Let him do it."

He was all scooted up on the edge of his chair, watching Donnie's every move. He looked excited like a little kid watching his grandma decorating Christmas cookies.

The safe was small and old. Not that high of quality.

"The hinges are the weak point. Just bash that fucker along the seams of the door till it pops out of the frame," I said.

Nick held up a hand at me, insisting on letting Donnie do his thing.

"Almost there," Donnie said, tweaking the dial.

Whatever. If they wanted to pretend that Donnie's taco assembling experience had somehow resulted in him acquiring safe-cracking skills, there's just not that much else to say about it.

Of course, Donnie also shushed me several times even though I wasn't making noise. I understand that a true safe whisperer such as himself needs absolute silence to work, though.

While we waited for Donnie to work his magic, Tammie made these smoothies called green monsters that were goddamn delicious. She held out a glass to me.

"What's in it?"

I eyed it somewhat suspiciously, it being green and all.

"It's like a couple frozen bananas, a scoop of peanut butter, a little Greek yogurt and a splash of almond milk topped with 2 huge handfuls of kale," she said.

Yes, kale, the cruciferous green vegetable.

I took a sip.

"Holy shit, this is awesome."

I know it sounds crazy, but it tastes good as hell. Aside from the thing being bright green, you wouldn't know that there was a salad or two worth of vegetables in there. I just tasted a delightful peanut butter and banana smoothie.

"Kale is like crazy good for you and reduces your risk of getting cancer like 60% or something, too," Tammie said. It turns out she is just full of useful information.

We sat on the couch watching the two fools work on the

safe.

"You know you guys are going to work forever on this," I said. "And there's probably nothing inside."

"You shut your mouth!" Donnie said.

He looked furious.

◆ ◆ ◆

I had a dream last night that I was back in the woman's bedroom. The lady. And I was waiting in the doorway, shining my light on her, except her hair was blond now. And she rolled over but kept her eyes closed. And it was Beth.

And I just watched her a while and listened to her breathe. She looked so peaceful. But it was weird, too. Somehow the fact that I was there made it obvious how not safe she was. I mean, it was just me, but it could have been anyone, you know. Someone else could sneak in there, and she'd be just as helpless and vulnerable.

She eventually kicked the blanket up and sighed and rolled over again. And I waited even longer, and watched and listened some more, and then I decided to go in for the jewelry box. But instead, without even thinking about it, I started climbing into the bed behind her, and then I woke up.

◆ ◆ ◆

I keep thinking about that old couple every so often. The people we robbed or whatever. I don't know. Part of me feels like I should feel sorry for them. Like putting a face to our victims should make me feel remorse or something, you know?

But I don't.

Maybe it's the stupid ben wa balls. Maybe it's something else. I don't care. I don't feel sorry. I took your safe. I won. Fuck you.

♦　　♦　　♦

Beth and I were in the Biology Lab. She volunteered to feed the rats for her biology teacher, so I followed her from cage to cage while she dropped a handful of rat food into each bowl. Rat food seems to be mostly comprised of a variety of seeds.

"I watched this dating show the other day," Beth said. "I can't remember what it was called."

"Love Connection?" I said.

"No. That one is ancient. This was newer."

She thought a minute.

"I guess it doesn't matter which one it was, really. At the beginning, though, they had the contestants, these four girls, do video interviews that the potential suitors watched. They could talk about whatever they wanted. To really emphasize the important qualities that make up who they are, right?"

"Right."

I handed Beth a rat treat from the bag I was holding, and she set it in the cage. The rat went straight for the treat and started munching away.

"This girl went on and on about how she is a feminist, but her ex-boyfriend used to open the door for her all the time anyway, which really bothered her."

"What?"

"No, really. That was her idea of what being a feminist is. A woman who doesn't want a guy to hold a door open for her. Under any circumstances. She mentioned it again when she got eliminated. She said the guy contestants must not want a girl that opens her own doors."

"That's funny."

Beth walked to the sink at the back of the room and squirted a pile of pink soap foam into her hands. She lathered.

"It made me think about this article I read, though, about how men find skinny women attractive not based solely on physical attraction, but the idea that a skinny woman is an obedient woman. You know? If she works out and watches what she eats to meet that social norm or expectation, she is obeying what men want, and that's part of why they like it."

"I guess that makes sense in a way."

"Yeah, in a way. And then breast implants are even more so. At that point the woman is going under the knife not only to obey men but to actually debase herself in a certain way solely to be sexually attractive to men, you know? It's no longer in any way a health issue or a grooming issue or anything like that. It's getting huge sex balloon things attached to your body. Willingly making yourself a toy for men. Humiliating yourself, and in a way some men like that."

Beth tore off a length of brown paper towel and dried her hands with it before wadding it up and tossing it in the garbage can.

"Yeah. Sheesh," I said.

"I don't know, though. It's all so complicated."

"Yeah, for real."

She was right. I honestly never thought boobs would seem so complicated.

CHAPTER 18

I WENT TO NICK'S AFTER school today. I could hear this weird hissing type sound as I climbed the steps on the porch. Somehow I knew Donnie was responsible.

I turned the corner to find Donnie and Nick both wearing welding masks. The hissing emitted from the blow torch in Donnie's hand which he was waving back and forth across the top of the safe. Little puffs of black smoke rolled off the spots where the flame touched the metal.

Nick flipped his welding mask up.

"Donnie figures that the top is the weak point," he said. "We're goin' to burn our way in."

He smiled and flipped the mask back down.

I didn't say anything. I just stood and watched for a few minutes and then turned to leave.

♦ ♦ ♦

Beth squinted and looked at the ceiling. I followed her gaze to a brown water stain that was sort of shaped like Idaho.

"I think I might be a little bit psychic," she said.

I smiled.

"Oh really?"

"Yeah! Like one time, when I was five, there was this contest for Halloween. You had to guess the weight of this insane pumpkin that was about the size of a Prius. My dad took me in and let me guess a number. And I was five, you know. I probably didn't know how much I weighed, let alone an enormous pumpkin."

She leaned in closer, and I could smell mint on her breath. She always seemed so clean somehow.

"I was four ounces off. Less than half a freaking pound!"

It suddenly struck me that the room had gone silent around us.

Shit.

I looked past Beth's shoulder to the front of the classroom, and sure enough, there was Mr. Burback: arms crossed, lips pursed, eyebrows arched in exaggerated annoyance, staring eyeball laser beams through the back of Beth's skull.

Beth hadn't noticed. She was still talking about the damn giant pumpkin.

"So obviously there's no logical explanation for it other than I'm psychic."

"Beth," I said it like a ventriloquist, my lips barely moving, my teeth all clenched. "Beth, turn around."

"What? Oh."

She glanced over her shoulder and sighed.

"Sorry," she said, and turned to face the front of the room.

I held my breath, and I liked to imagine that the rest of the class did the same. I almost think it's worse when you're anticipating trouble for someone else somehow. Like if Mr. Burback was winding up to yell at me, I might even think it was kind of funny, but I was terrified on Beth's behalf for whatever reason. Anyway, it was the moment of truth.

Mr. Burback tapped his toe a couple times and then held still. For a second, I thought he was going to let it go. But no.

"Oh no, please. Don't let me interrupt your conversation," he said.

He liked to lay the sarcasm on as thick as his mustache.

"Go ahead. Please finish, I'm sure it's very important. You can let me know when you're done."

He did this same routine about 50% of the time someone didn't stop "socializing" (His word, not mine. Douche.) the instant he demanded the class's attention. At some point Beth pointed out that he was more apt to direct it at the girls than the guys, and I'm pretty sure she's right. So he's a sexist douche, apparently.

Now Beth would stare at her shoes, and bite her lip, and whisper, "No, I'm done. Sorry." And sink a little lower in her seat. I've read that humiliation is a very effective teaching method.

Instead, however, Beth cocked her head to one side.

"Oh, okay then." She said it with extra pep and a cheesy smile to match his overdone sarcasm.

She swiveled around to face me.

"Anyway... what was I saying before? Oh yeah. The pumpkin."

I think my jaw actually dropped. No one had ever attempted this before.

I looked up at Mr. Burback. He looked... insane. Absolutely insane with rage. Face beet red, nostrils flaring.

He jabbed a finger at Beth.

"Alright! Out!"

Beth raised her eyebrows and shrugged as she grabbed her books.

"Both of you! Out!"

I opened my mouth to protest. Me? I hadn't done anything. But then I thought the better of it for a variety of reasons. One: I didn't like the prospects of arguing with Mr. Burback in the midst of his 'roid rage. Two: I would look like a huge puss. Three: As fascinating as listening to Mr. Mustache lecture the class on the economic hardships in the post-Civil War South might be, sitting with Beth in the hallway unsupervised might be OK, too.

I picked up my books and followed Beth out of the room.

The door closed behind us, and there was a moment of total silence. Then we both started laughing. We were both scared of making too much noise and further enraging Mr. Burback, so we kind of tried to hold the laughing back, and that just made us laugh even harder. Our laughs echoed down the hall.

When I finally caught my breath, I said, "Dude, that was awesome."

"Did you see his face?" she said.

"His mustache was quivering with rage."

"Yeah well, I'm sick of his crap. He thinks he's so cool."

Beth plopped onto the cool brown floor.

"He just gets off on bullying and humiliating people. Oh, except the girls that sit in the front row. They get a free pass because he gets to look down their shirts when they pretend to laugh at his stupid jokes. Fucking pervert loser."

"I don't know if I've ever seen a teacher get that mad. He was homicidal."

Beth crossed one knee over the other and dangled her shoe off the end of her foot.

"It was weird. For a split second, I almost did what everyone else does. Like cower and say, 'Oh no, Mr. Burback,

I'm so sorry, please forgive me.' But something welled up inside me and was like, 'Nope. Not this time, fucker.' And I just went for it."

♦   ♦   ♦

I lugged a sledgehammer over to Nick's today. Donnie was attempting to drill a hole into the front of the safe just above the dial with an orange Black and Decker drill. That maybe would've eventually worked if he spent about 1,000 years and a bunch of drill bits working on it. Maybe.

They hadn't really noticed me come in, so I let the sledgehammer rest on the floor. Loudly. The drilling stopped, and their heads turned.

"Let's try it my way," I said.

They both immediately looked all pissed off.

"Donnie's drillin'," Nick said. "This'll work. You just relax."

"Look, you and Donnie have been dicking around with this damn thing for days. Give me an hour."

Donnie huffed.

"Fine," he said and tossed his drill to the floor.

Nick sighed. I got him to help me lay the safe down face up. Then he held the wedge in the top right corner of the opening while I tapped it in enough that it would stay put on its own. Now the sledging commenced. I bashed at it a while, with the wedge progressing slowly and steadily. Weirdly, my forehead seemed to sweat more than anywhere else. I paused to wipe it and Nick pried at the door a little.

"It's got a little give to it," he said. "A little."

"Just wait," I said.

We put another wedge in the bottom right corner and repeated the process. I swung the hammer until my arms felt dead, but by then Nick was asking to take a turn. He seemed to have grown more optimistic. Even Donnie had a hopeful look about him.

Forty-seven minutes after we started, the door busted off the hinges. Actually, the hinges busted off the frame, and the door sort of fell into the safe a little. Some kind of weird white powder came out of the holes into the innards of the safe wall. Silica or something, I guess.

Donnie and Nick jumped up and down like kids. And nobody moved to pull the door free. It was weird. I think somehow we all wanted to delay the process of revealing what was inside. Just for a moment.

"How did you know that would work?" Donnie said.

"I don't know. It was a crappy safe. This probably wouldn't have worked with a good one."

"Nah, dude," Donnie said. "You're bein' modest. That was the shit."

♦ ♦ ♦

Nick peeled the door out from the hinge side, wiggled it to loosen it up and pried it open about six inches. Donnie skittered over to peek inside. They just hovered over it for a moment, so I moved closer.

"What is it?" I said.

Inside was a gigantic double-sided dildo rippled with veins.

CHAPTER 19

I HAD A DREAM LAST night that I trudged through this endless marsh. Ankle-deep water. Lily pads everywhere. Algae and stuff. Some of those mangrove trees or whatever popped up here and there, with the mess of exposed roots at the bottom and thick wads of moss hanging down from the branches.

Fog misted in all directions, so I could only see 15 or 20 feet in front of me. Everything seemed to have a blue tint to it, too. Even the air.

I was running from something. I don't know what it was. I couldn't see anything behind me, but I was scared. My feet kicked through the sludgy water. My chest heaved hot, fighting to not lose my breath.

The water got deeper, almost to my knees. I was slowing down. And then a clear spot appeared before me, a break in the mist, and I could see a figure face down in the bog.

A girl.

Long blond hair swirled on the rippling surface of the water around her submerged head. I turned her over, and it was Beth, and she immediately coughed up a bunch of water. Brown water. Projectile style.

So I gathered her in my arms to carry her, but her face went white with fear. Her eyes bugged out. She was scared of me. Hysterically so. Her tiny fists pounded at my chest as I ran. She spoke no words, but she screeched periodically and thrashed in my arms, though I was too strong for her, thankfully.

It hurt. Not the fists. Just her being scared of me hurt. Like my feelings or whatever. Somehow I wasn't mad at her, though, 'cause I knew she was just confused. I knew she would forgive me once she understood that I was protecting her.

We splashed on, and she started to relax. The water grew shallower and shallower. The lily pads thinned out. Soon, I could see a rocky shore sloping up in front of me. I stomped onto the land, the water still squishing inside of my shoes.

As I topped the hill of the shoreline, a field of tall grass spread out in front of me. I could see a rock wall in the distance, and the mouth of a cave dead ahead. I knew we would be safe there somehow.

My pace quickened. The grass brushed at my legs. Fire and sandpaper ripped at my lungs, but I didn't care anymore. I sprinted the last fifty feet.

I laid her down on a bed of pine needles in the half-light of the cave. She was really peaceful now. Actually, I thought she might be asleep. She sat up, though, to kiss me on the cheek, and I knew she forgave me, and I knew she loved me. Whatever was out there couldn't get us now.

◆　◆　◆

In the locker room before gym, I saw Chad Walters talking to Robert. He's this wrestler kid that's all short with big tree trunk legs and teeth that look like kernels of corn. I didn't think much of it until I saw all of Chad's friends crowded behind him laughing.

I moved closer.

"You don't know whether you've jerked off or not?" Chad

said. He flashed his corn cob smile.

"What's that?" Robert said.

"Shut up, Chad," I said.

He didn't acknowledge my presence.

"Well, you take your hand like this and—"

He pantomimed a jerking off motion in the air.

"—stroke it up and down the shaft of—"

At that point his words cut off into a series of gurgled choking noises, because I had punched him in the throat as hard I could. He tottered forward slightly, so I gave him a shove on the back of the shoulder that helped him belly flop down onto the tiled floor. I kicked him in the ribs so he would stay down a while.

He did.

One of his friends, Steve Smallwood, took half a step toward me, but I just glared at him, and he left it at that.

When I looked back at Robert, though, he looked really scared of me. He wouldn't say anything.

♦ ♦ ♦

I went straight to Nick's after school today. Rain squirted down on me, so I had to run the last two blocks. Nick was home alone, sitting on the recliner and staring out the window at the wet street. He looked agitated.

"You know how there's all that shit out there tryin' to make everyone feel guilty for downloadin' music and movies?"

"Yeah."

"And they talk about how much it hurts the artists and all that?"

"Right."

"Well, it's hilarious that the corporations try to pull that shit. Really hilarious. Because they rip off the artists all the goddamn time."

He scratched his nose.

"Remember how successful those *Lord of the Rings* movies were?"

"Yes."

"New Line Cinema gave the J.R.R. Tolkien estate $62,500 for the rights to make the *Lord of the Rings* movies, and they were supposed to give 7.5% of whatever the movies made. The movies have made $6 billion and the company never paid the Tolkien estate another cent. They had to sue. Same with the guy that wrote the book *Forrest Gump*. It made $700 million at the box office and who knows how much in DVD sales and merchandise, and they told him it didn't profit and paid him zero royalties, so he refused to sell them the rights to the sequel."

Nick shook his head, frowning slightly.

"It happens in music, too. Might be worse, even. The point is, it's the same as everything else. They want one set of rules for the idiot masses — no stealing — and another set of rules for the people at the top — steal as much as you can get away with."

He didn't quite seem to be talking to me so much as at me, so I didn't say anything. Just sat there and let him go on.

"It's like that in every industry, in every facet of life now. The agribusiness corporations fix the scales to rip off the farmers and soak the grain with water to run up the prices before they sell it. Factories and plants keep fake injury logs to show to OSHA inspectors. And don't even get me started on the Wall Street banks and all the shit they've pulled."

He paused and rubbed at the stubble on his chin.

"When you boil it all down, there are no real rules. Just don't get caught. That's the only rule."

We fell silent, with only the sounds of cars sludging through mud puddles outside surrounding us. My eyes fell on a drinking glass on the coffee table. It was crusted with what appeared to be the mummified remains of a green monster smoothie. I was pretty sure it was the glass I'd used the day Donnie was trying to open the safe with the stethoscope. That was like over a week ago. Gross.

"Where's Tammie?" I said.

Nick's gaze fell to the floor.

"She wound up movin' away," he said.

"Really? Just like that?"

"Yeah. Moved to Ohio with her Aunt or something."

CHAPTER 20

IT'S WEIRD HOW, ON THEIR own, each side of the brain seems pretty dumb. I was thinking about this phenomenon of the left brain overdoing the order thing. I mean, that is its role. It organizes the information. It learns from the pattern of events that have happened and applies what it learns to predicting the future. But sometimes it oversimplifies things.

Like when the football team at school wins, everyone gets overconfident and assumes they will win the next game and all of the remaining games. People start talking about "going to state."(I mean, like, the playoffs or whatever.) When they lose, everyone panics and assumes they will lose the next game and all of the rest, too.

It's like this weird oversimplified order that our left brain tries to impose upon everything. It can't comprehend the unknown. It hates the idea of not knowing what will happen next. It won't acknowledge that there is a randomness — a chaos — to football games. Sports are unpredictable, and that's why there are so many upsets and so forth. The left brain wants to believe that all history can do is repeat the same results over and over, because recognizing patterns is how it understands the world.

The right brain, on the other hand, is more likely to be responsible for completely irrational behavior, which is equally dumb, I suppose. Like when people commit crimes on a whim. They've done studies with brain scans that show criminals get these spikes of activity in their right brain frequently. We're talking like an off-the-charts type spike. So they get this tidal wave of an impulse and wind up stealing a car or whatever. The irrational urge takes over their behavior and lands them in prison eventually. If they would just weigh the consequences, they wouldn't do it, but the irrational right brain wins out.

I don't know. Together the two sides of the brain can work pretty well at times, but separately they are pretty screwy, I think. They are incomplete.

◆　◆　◆

I walked home with Beth after school. She asked me to. The plan was not to actually hang out at her house or anything, though. She had to get ready to go to some play with her mom right after school, I guess. So the actual walk — moving from point A to point B — was the thing we would be doing together. She said she wanted to talk. The old fashioned walk and talk, you know?

I met her in the parking lot behind the school. She was wearing a light blue shirt with puff sleeves. (Did I already mention that her boobs are huge? I think I did.) She seemed to be in a pretty good mood.

We headed due West... or maybe a different direction. I'm not like a cartographer or something.

We walked along this bike-slash-nature trail. It's an asphalt path that's really only like fifteen feet from the road most of the way, but it's surrounded by woods and everything. You feel like you have a little more privacy, I guess. On the downside, you periodically get whiffs of like a pond scum smell. But other

151

than that, it's pretty relaxing. After we exchanged the "How was your day?" type crap, we got down to business.

"So you remember the other day," she said. "When I was all upset?"

"I do."

"And I told you I would tell you some other time what was the matter?"

"I remember."

"Well, I wanted to tell you about it today."

I waited for her to spill it, but she didn't say anything. After a while she sniffled.

"Are you OK?" I said.

"Yeah. Well, in some ways."

Just then a bell rang and a voice called out from behind us.

"On your left!"

A guy on a bike whizzed past on our left. I guess that was his warning call, but there was something too obnoxious about it. I mean, I get that ultimately he was being helpful, but I still got a powerful urge to throw a rock at him or something.

Besides, what's the deal with how like every douche on a bike these days has to dress up in a full Lance Armstrong costume? Is it seriously necessary for everyone to wear a brightly colored spandex unitard or whatever just to ride around town on a goddamn bicycle?

"I'm bulimic," she said.

This caught me off guard, although there were probably things I should have picked up on. Like the long bathroom break at the movies and everything. Yep. A cycle of binging and purging, dude. Pretty gross.

"Really?" I said.

"Really. I have been for three years."

"Doesn't that, like, erode the hell out of your esophagus and teeth and stuff?"

(Not to mention the constant puke breath.)

"It can. It can cause all kinds of problems."

(Puke breath. Among other ailments.)

I had no goddamn idea what to say. Do you say "sorry" or what? I mean, you could say "Well, please stop being bulimic and anorexic and stuff. Chew. Swallow. Don't vomit. 'K, thanks." It probably wouldn't help anything, though.

"For a long time, I didn't want to admit it, but I guess at some point you have to."

"Right. Well, that's the first step, you know. Admitting you have a problem."

Nerdy. Such a nerdy thing to say. Dr. Phil would know just what to say, and he would deliver it with an authoritative twang. Meanwhile Dr. Oz would use a big papier-mâché colon to show us how bulimia affects our poop.

She grabbed my arm and hugged it against her.

"I know you'll help me get through it."

And I will. It's weird. Here in this journal I kind of detach from things. When I am there with her, I feel differently. Reading through this, you might even think that I don't like her or whatever, 'cause I'm sarcastic and everything, but I do. I really do.

I don't know. It's complicated.

"Have you told your mom and dad?" I said.

Her brow furrowed.

"Not yet. Maybe I never will."

"Well, are you talking to, like, a professional about it?"

"Yeah. I'm in therapy."

"That's good."

We walked past a guy on rollerblades walking a couple of dogs. (Do you still call it walking a dog if the human is on rollerblades? And what if the dogs are on rollerblades? Additionally, who the hell rollerblades these days? Christ.)

One dog was a pug, who mainly seemed interested in pushing his face into the leaves along the side of the trail. The other looked like a pit bull/boxer mix that expressed less interest in the plant life and more interested in ripping my damn face off. For real.

He locked eyes with me from far away, and his head perked up. As we passed, he did a lurch and growl at me, but the rollerblader managed to hold him back, which seemed impressive considering the neon green wheels on his feet.

Dogs hate me. I don't get it, but a lot of them want to bite and/or maim me for some reason. The big ones, especially. I told Nick about it once, and he laughed.

"Well, dogs are great judges of character," he said. "Nah, seriously. They can pick up on your nature, and they're threatened for some reason. They think you're dangerous."

He kept a fairly straight face, but he had to be messing with me, right? Who says "You're dangerous!" and means it? It's too silly.

Beth and I went back to talking about normal things after that. She said she got an A on her biology test and that her cousin was going to Germany as an exchange student for a semester, but, honestly, all I could think about the whole time was her puking up a bunch of veal chunks and yogurt and blue Powerade and egg salad and stuff.

♦   ♦   ♦

So I've been reading about the psychology of bulimia and other eating disorders. I bet you can't guess what it's all about. Stumped, right? Control. Every goddamn thing is about control, I think. Sheesh.

People with eating disorders feel out of control of their own lives for various reasons — lack of connection, feeling betrayed, fear of life, anger, self-hatred, etc. — and so they start to gain a sense of power over themselves by getting super controlling over what they eat. Most are hung up on looks and skinniness, of course, so not eating (or barfing it all up) becomes the goal. Not just the goal, actually, it becomes the obsession.

A lot of them have controlling parents who sort of deny their identity. I'll admit that Beth's mom did seem like a huge cuntburger, too. About the ice cream, I mean. (Is cuntburger a real term, or did I just make it up? Can I get a confirmation on this?)

Anyway, that's pretty sad. I mean, think about how they feel so strongly that their parent is denying their identity that they make themselves vomit almost as a way of claiming that they deserve to exist at all. It's proof that they're an individual, and they have control over at least one thing in the universe. Puking is the way they stand up for themselves. On some level, that is the underlying psychological state of the thing. Very odd.

And what is it inside of us that is perpetually drawn to extremes like that? These people with these issues never say, "I'm going to take control of my life by eating a well-balanced diet and slowly but surely reaching my ideal weight by doing this the right way." They say, "I'm going to pig out and then jam my finger down my throat in a little bit." We're just so quick to have this air of desperation to so many of the things we do.

Maybe it's all connected. Like the people lining up for the iPads are desperately looking for meaning in their lives. Maybe it's the same with the bulimics and anorexics. Maybe looking for a meaning that's not there is the desperation that drives us all, and we all have different ways of showing it and dealing with it.

CHAPTER 21

PARTY IS A WEIRD WORD 'cause it can mean so many different things.

I went to a party with Nick and Donnie tonight. Their version of a party apparently entails a bunch of dudes, mostly, and a few girls, in a second-floor studio apartment downtown above a barber shop. Ages ranged from 25-ish to 40-ish with me being the one exception (until later, anyway). Household incomes ranged from $0 to $14,000 annually, I'm guessing. The dental hygiene ranged from fair to very poor. The dress code was casual.

We walked into the apartment. A small group of adults stood around a pony keg of Labatt Blue that was squatting in the kitchen.

A party of younger kids has an air of enthusiasm and excitement as their futures are wide open in front of them. This one? Not so much. I guess you could say it had an air of schwag weed and unpaid child support.

Let's not mince words. These people are members of the underclass, and not the sympathetic, down-on-their-luck types. The full-on criminals. Some of them can't read. Most of them don't read. All of them are addicted to booze or drugs or both.

I decided not to drink. You've got to keep your wits about you in the presence of this kind of company, right? I walked around the party to watch all the people.

Two 40-year-old men took turns with a beer bong in the

kitchen area while two other gentlemen argued about NASCAR. One wore a trucker hat while the other sported a t-shirt with the sleeves scissored off.

"There ain't no way he'll beat Jimmie Johnson in wins," Trucker Hat said.

"Yeah, but those pussies are just lucky that Dale Earnhardt, Sr. isn't around anymore. He'd wipe the floor with their asses," Sleeveless said.

I also heard one guy expound upon the price of a "pound of dope wholesale" and toss out some mental math returns on how much you could make by dividing it up for retail.

Spots on the couch became a valued commodity. Vulture types circled patiently, and the second someone got up to go to the bathroom or refill their cup, the birds of prey swooped in to claim their seat. Harsh words were exchanged a time or two as you might imagine, but possession is nine-tenths of all seating law.

No matter where I turned, though, I couldn't avoid the gaze of a scrawny guy with a mohawk and a big chain around his neck. Not like a jewelry chain. A dog chain. His face was all emaciated like someone in an AIDs ward, and his eyes had that perpetually paranoid wide open all the time look. I bet he could go days without blinking. He seemed to be watching me, which I did not, you must understand, care for.

Donnie hunched by the stereo, his arm around some pear-shaped girl's waist. He whispered into her ear. Nick milled around with some guys in the hallway leading to the bathroom. I had my shoulders squared away from the mohawk creep, so I didn't see him approaching me.

"What's your deal?" he said, dangerously close to my ear.

There is something unsettling about someone sneaking up behind you. And yet I placed his voice right away as the one I'd heard detailing the in and outs of "slangin' a pound of dope." I wheeled to face him. He was about six inches shorter than me, so I stared down at him, our faces a little too close for comfort.

"What?" I said.

"I said what's your deal?" he said.

I didn't say anything. I've reached a point in my life where I no longer feel obliged to answer nonsense questions. I did note that his front teeth were stained with chocolatey swirls, and the molars visible from the sides of his mouth were rotting away like crazy.

"Who the fuck are you?" he said.

"I'm Jake," I said.

I would've asked who the hell he was, but, frankly, I didn't want to know this guy. Why would I ever want to? Maybe if I had questions about scabies or something, I could contact this person and get the details straightened out. He could recommend ointments and such.

"Jake, huh?" he said.

We stared at each other for a silent moment.

"Yeah," I said.

He laughed through a grimace of rotting teeth.

"Shit. I can tell just by lookin' at ya that you ain't nothin' but trouble," he said.

I shrugged.

"You know someone here or what?" he said.

I nodded toward Nick.

"I'm Nick's cousin."

His eyes shifted over to Nick and back. He did a double-take, and the faintest flinch shook his frame. The actual movement was subtle, yet I picked up on it so clearly. Like the air around him changed. He glanced back at me and quickly broke eye contact, his gaze sweeping to the floor.

"Ah, that's cool," he said, and he walked off.

Whatever. I slid open the sliding glass door to squeeze onto the small balcony where the hoards of smokers huddled. Nothing like fresh, carcinogenic air. I was leaning on the wrought iron rail when Nick came up beside me. He took a long drink from his Dixie cup and mopped beer foam off of his top lip with the collar of his t-shirt.

"So what did Dildo Sucker want?" he said.

"What?"

"Dildo Sucker. I saw him talkin' to you in there. What did he want?"

"You mean the mohawk guy?"

"Yeah."

"People call him Dildo Sucker?"

"Yeah. Well, I mean, I do."

"What's that all about?"

"He owed me money and kept avoidin' me, so I started gettin' people to prank call him and tell him that we all know that he sucks on dildos. Stuff like that."

"Makes sense," I said, but it didn't. "He asked me what my deal was, and then he left me alone."

Nick nodded and took another drink.

◆　◆　◆

"Can you say?!" is one of my least favorite clichés. Like if a football team intercepts a pass, some douchebag watching the game has to say:

"Can you say *interception*?!"

No. But I can say, "Shut the fuck up, cocksucker."

v

The party dragged on for hours. Most of the activities stayed the same but slowed down. Literally, I mean. The topics of conversation remained in the same realm, but everyone's speech got slurred. The party-goers' motor skills got slower and stumblier. Reaction times? You guessed it. Real fuckin' slow.

Later on some high school kids showed up. (Three guys. No one that I recognized from school or anything, but you could tell they were young, you know?) The keg was empty, but someone was giving these kids wine coolers, which seemed funny in a way. Three dudes drinking Bahama Mama flavored wine coolers. (Fine. I guess now I get why Donnie was so amused by the Strawberry Hill.)

Some arm wrestling led to a shoving match among the guys who were debating NASCAR earlier, so I kind of lost track of these high school kids for a while. When I next noticed them, they were in the bathtub, taking turns making out with this 38-year-old woman that I'd met earlier named Meg. (Needless to say, Meg has a number of issues.)

It was repulsive. I mean, I really wanted to tell them to stop it. But then I thought about it. Nobody else here cared. Why should I care? Right? Why should it bother me so much to see these underage strangers making out with a middle-aged woman? It's not like I object all that strongly on moral grounds or anything.

And then I realized that it was my right brain reacting, like animal instincts kicking in, 'cause this is potentially bad for the species. Meg has problems. Do not mate with Meg. I repeat, do not mate with Meg!

♦　♦　♦

I had a dream that I was lying in bed, and a wolf charged at me. Instinctively, I grabbed the snout and jaw and kept the immense fangs pried apart. And it thrashed its head around, trying to shake free to kill me. But I somehow knew the whole time that it had the capacity to be a nice wolf. Like there was no malice in its actions, you know? It's just a wolf. A wild animal. It didn't know any better.

I held the jaw open for a long time, and then I woke up.

CHAPTER 22

THE GYM TEACHER UNLOCKED THE ball closet and stepped out of view into the dark cavern. A series of basketballs flew out onto the gym floor. They bounced in all directions as the students swarmed like insects to collect them. Once the proper number of balls were unleashed, Mr. Smith emerged from his ball cave.

"Pair up and pick a hoop," he said. "We're working on free throws today."

The students zigged and zagged all around, basketballs thudded on the floor, and the growing murmur of the collective voices took the place of the silence that had been there a moment before.

A whistle blew. The silence returned. Mr. Smith raised his hand to further command our attention.

"One more thing," he said. "No hanging on the nets today to pull yourself up and dunk it. It stretches 'em out and ruins 'em. I'm looking at you, Koontz."

Billy Koontz grinned with embarrassment.

"Go on," Mr. Smith said, letting his hand drop to his side.

I moved toward Robert, but he wouldn't look at me. He hadn't talked to me in a couple weeks, but that couldn't last forever, could it?

As I opened my mouth to ask if we'd be partners like we always were, he tapped Billy Koontz on the shoulder, nodded at him, and they moved away from me toward the hoop in the far corner.

♦ ♦ ♦

So I read about this product called the Thundershirt. It's this fabric that you wrap and strap around your dog that provides constant gentle pressure to the animal's torso. This synthetic hug eases their stress and anxiety from the sound of thunder or separation from their owner. Pretty much all anxiety. It's 80% effective. Kinda crazy.

It kind of boils things down in a weird way. This simple mammal has a button you can press that reduces its anxiety no matter what. Let's call it the hug button. You put this fabric on the dog, it presses the hug button, and they calm down. Totally nuts.

But we're mammals, too, right? Aren't we probably the same? Do we have ridiculously simple stimulus buttons of our own like that? I think we must.

They cost like $40. The Thundershirts, I mean. That's for the black. I think it's more to get a fancy color.

♦ ♦ ♦

So reading up further, some autistic people use this thing called a hug machine. They find it difficult to turn to other people for affection, and they actually can find hugging a real person to be overstimulating, so they developed this machine they sit in, and it squeezes them. This relaxes them and relieves their stress. Some use the machine on a daily basis. It basically replaces physical affection from other people altogether.

And it's an old invention. I think it predates the damn Thundershirt by decades.

That's pretty weird, though. I mean, it makes sense, but it's still hard to believe it would work for a person in a way.

CHAPTER 23

NICK DOESN'T ACTUALLY DRINK THAT often, interestingly enough. When he does, though, he is completely out of control.

I went to his apartment after school today, and he was, indeed, quite drunk. It was uncomfortable. Donnie and I just sat there while he ranted and raved and was generally a total dick to both of us.

"You're like thirty, and you work at Taco Bell. Serving your dog meat tacos to big fatties all day long," he slurred at Donnie. "Fuckin' pathetic."

Spit flew out of Nick's mouth when he laughed.

But we couldn't leave. Or at least that's how I felt. I felt like he would be offended if I left or something and might become hostile. Or more hostile than he already was, I guess.

He chain-smoked the whole time and kept taking big swigs out of this half-gallon bottle of Jim Beam. His face was all shiny.

"Buncha pussies," he said. He didn't explain any kind of context for the sentence fragment. I assumed he was calling Donnie and me pussies, but who knows?

Donnie gave me a glance, and then the two of us went back to staring at the floor without saying anything. I traced my finger along the seam running up the side of my jeans.

Nick took another slug off of the Jim Beam, and two rivers of whiskey poured down from the corners of his mouth and onto his shirt. He wiped his wrist across his mouth, effectively smearing the bourbon over most of his face.

"Someday you pussies will turn on the TV and see me on there. And you'll be all like, 'Damn. That's Nick. I used to know that fuggin' guy.'"

He fidgeted in his chair a moment and everything got quiet. Awkward.

"Ain't that right, Donnie?"

"Yep."

"Ain't that shit right?"

"It's right."

He sat back in his chair. His neck slackened, and his head drooped back onto the headrest. He closed his eyes. Donnie looked at me with raised eyebrows. I shrugged.

I heard the grind and click of a Bic lighter, and when I looked back at Nick, he was setting an envelope on fire. He was burning the damn mail.

"What the hell?" Donnie said.

He sprang from his chair and tore the letter from Nick's hand. Flames flickered along the edge of the paper, so Donnie tossed it to the floor and stomped it out.

"What is wrong with you?" Donnie said.

Nick just laughed. I picked the envelope up and saw that it was actually a piece of Tammie's mail. (Tamra Mooney. I had never known her full name before that.) It still had her old address and everything, but it was post-marked for yesterday's date which didn't seem right.

"Are you picking up Tammie's mail for her or something?" I said.

"Yeah," Nick said. He was still smiling, but he didn't look

right somehow. I mean, he seemed tense all of a sudden.

"So you're going to forward it to her in Ohio?" I said.

"I think he plans to incinerate it for her," Donnie said.

Nick laughed again.

"She doesn't need all that mail," he said. "Believe me."

It didn't really make sense, but he was so drunk, you know? It probably wasn't worth trying to sort it all out just then.

Nick grabbed the little lever on the side of his chair and un-reclined suddenly. He pushed himself to his feet.

"Let's go," he said and headed for the door.

Donnie glanced at me out of the corner of his eye.

"Where are we going?"

Nick scoffed, like it was obvious or something.

"To the Hunt Club."

The Hunt Club is like this bar-slash-restaurant with taxidermied animal heads lining the walls. Mostly hooved beasts — deer, caribou, elk, boar and so on. It's not exactly a rowdy place. In fact, it usually draws an older crowd, but Nick managed to start trouble anyway.

We walked in and Nick pretty much immediately rammed his elbow into the back of a white-haired guy at the bar. In fairness, I think Nick was just trying to push his way to the front, but he really blasted this guy, and the old man dumped a beer all over himself. Nick didn't seem to realize he'd bumped anyone. He felt the need, however, to chime in once he noticed that the old guy's shirt was wet and frothy.

"Watch where you're going, fag," he said.

All class.

Next, we overheard a tall guy telling his friends that he was making a scrapbook for this girl that he had a crush on.

"Now that we're finally going out, I just want to put something together that tells the story of how we met and how long we've known each other," he said.

Nick chimed in again.

"I'd probably think that was creepy as hell," he said. He wasn't just talking directly to the guy but yelling across the room to him. "If some weirdo made a scrapbook about how long he'd been stalkin' me or whatever for our first date. I wouldn't like that if I was a girl. I'd be gettin' a damn restrainin' order."

The guy's cheeks went all red. His friends looked mad, but they also looked a little intimidated by Nick. Rightfully so, I suppose. These were office workers with the baby soft hands that come with never doing a day of manual labor in one's life.

It went on like this with Nick confronting and annoying people, until he finally pushed a bald guy down by the jukebox.

A few minutes later, the manager came over.

"I'm going to need you gentlemen to leave before I call the cops."

Nick sized him up for a moment, but the guy was pretty burly, so ultimately we left without further incident.

I realized somewhere in there that I'd never seen Nick let go like this before. He's usually very under control of his demeanor and all of that. I mean, he's a cold, calculating thief, really. Getting all drunk and obnoxious like this didn't seem right. It didn't fit the guy that was teaching me this screwed up philosophy or whatever the hell he was teaching me.

Maybe that's why he doesn't do it often, I guess. It seems most ridiculous to suggest that I saw something of his dark side or something like that, 'cause let's face it, this guy doesn't exactly have a light side. Still, there was something ugly about it. He let his underlying emotions bubble to the surface, and it turns out what's hiding down there is this immature, impulsive bully. Is that like his real self? Not sure. In any case, he let it out a little bit tonight, and I didn't like it.

And that observation was as close as I got to a lesson this week.

♦ ♦ ♦

In Psychology today we talked about impulse control disorders. Basically at all times our brain is sending out these impulses. Some of which we're very conscious of. Others emit from places in the right brain that our conscious mind doesn't really have access to. They all affect our thoughts and behavior, either way.

So an impulse is like a little signal that gives you the urge to do something. Some are pretty normal: An impulse to eat. An impulse to have sex (and reproduce). Some are conditioned responses that people learn based on their behavior: A nicotine addict will get an impulse to smoke. An alcoholic gets the urge to drink. And so on.

But there are violent impulses coming out of there, too. An impulse to strike someone you're mad at. Stuff like that. And most of the time, most people can control these impulses. They can sort of withstand that initial draw to behave a certain way because they can reason out the negative long term effects. Essentially, they can think, "I shouldn't punch this guy in the face. I will go to jail. If I just let it go, I won't go to jail." Or, "I shouldn't drink. I have to drive home, and I don't want to get arrested or get in a wreck."

But there are people with these disorders, various kinds of "overlapping neural circuits" or something, that make them unable to reason it out. They find it difficult to resist the impulses. It sort of makes them more prone to get addicted to stuff, having their brains wired this way. Some people think it's genetic and call it the addiction gene.

There are even people with brain damage that have very little impulse control at all. So these crazy ideas pop into their heads and they have to act upon them. There's no real filter there. They just do the things that occur to them. Sort of thoughtlessly wandering through life.

Wouldn't that be a crazy way to live?

♦　♦　♦

Robert still won't talk to me. I think he is done with me.

♦　♦　♦

In the Netherlands they have this Christmas tradition where Santa goes around with his trusty sidekick Zwarte Piet. Now, these days, Zwarte Piet is a loveable doofus type character, kind of aloof, I guess, to amuse the kids. I should probably explain that the direct translation of Zwarte Piet is Black Peter. And he is always played by a white Dutch person in full blackface makeup.

In.

Goddamn.

Sane.

This still goes on today. Like I sort of explained, outside of the blackface aspect, it's fairly tame now, but it wasn't always that way.

Originally Zwarte Piet was evil and dumb. Santa used to beat him with a stick. A stick! Old Sinterklaas, as the people of Holland call him, was generally pretty rough with the bad kids all the way around, which is incredibly creepy. They used to sing songs about how Santa and Black Pete would shove the bad kids in a burlap sack and take them off to Spain. Good times.

In the 1800s, though, they changed things up and made the whole thing all lighthearted and everything.

Still, what the fuck? Elves with sweet toys weren't good enough? Sheesh.

◆   ◆   ◆

Today I got a firsthand glimpse of the Mean Girl Phenomenon that Beth was telling me about. We were eating lunch and Bree McIntosh and Tess Pulju walked by our table. Right as Bree passed behind Beth, she made this exaggerated puking/gagging sound. Like, "bluu-EHH!"

Tess snorted (in a most unladylike fashion, I might add), and she and Bree walked away laughing. Actually, it was more cackling than laughing. Definitely a witchy cackle thing going on there.

Beth stabbed at her salad with percussive little motions. She speared a piece of broccoli and aggressively swished it in the little cup of ranch before shoving it in her mouth.

"What was that all about?" I said.

"Oh, that's their newest joke," Beth said, shaking her head and forcing a wad of lettuce past her teeth. "Isn't it hilarious?"

I swirled a French fry around in the puddle of ketchup on my tray.

"Did you... I mean... How do they know?"

Beth swallowed and raised her eyebrows at me.

"That I'm bulimic?"

She looked back down at her salad and poked at a slice of cucumber.

"I told Stacey Peterson a long time ago, and I guess she must have blabbed about it."

She flipped the cucumber slice over.

"Stupid cow. I never should have trusted her and her big stupid cow mouth," she said and drove her fork through the cucumber so hard that it went all the way through the cuke and got stuck in the styrofoam tray.

I think what I found weirdest was how indirect it all was. They didn't stop or look at Beth. If I hadn't heard Beth mention their names specifically when she talked about them before, I don't know if I would have picked up on it being directed at her. When a guy like Troy Summers bullies you, it's totally in your face. But these girls... it was like they were bullying in secret code.

And even though they didn't touch her at all, it kind of seemed meaner than the way guys do it.

♦　♦　♦

I bet sliced smoked sausage wouldn't be a terrible pizza topping.

♦   ♦   ♦

Thursday after school, I went with Beth to the library so she could get some books for a paper she has to write for Biology. We walked through this little park in the middle of town on the way.

"I was reading about eating disorders on the internet today," she said. "And this website kept saying that eating disorders are very difficult to treat."

"Yeah?" I said.

"Yeah. Something about that pissed me off. Maybe it was partially the context. There was a defeatist, sympathetic tone to it, sort of like, 'good luck with all that.'"

"I get what you mean," I said.

A robin hopped across the grass in front of us. It stopped and plucked a worm from the ground before hopping away.

"But it made me realize that I have a lot more fight to me than I thought I did," she said. "Left by myself, it's easy to feel powerless, you know? To feel stuck."

She raked her fingers through a tangle in her hair before continuing.

"Once somebody else suggests I'm powerless, though? I'm all like 'Fuck you! What do you know about me? I can change myself.'"

She looked at me.

"It reminds me of things you've talked about. Like about bullies and people trying to control each other. Well, you can't control the world, but you can control yourself. You can change yourself. We're not all just powerless and trapped in the roles we find ourselves in. We can change."

CHAPTER 24

I DREAMED THAT I WAS at school, but the building was empty. Vacant hallways stretched out in all directions. Silence enveloped me. I messed with my locker for a long time, but no matter what I did, I couldn't get it to stay closed. I was pretty sure all my books were going to get stolen.

Then this gurgling static sound faded in around me. The sounds lurched and swayed, increasing in volume and echoing down the corridor. It seemed like if I listened to it hard enough, I could make out these tones, almost like a distorted keyboard, playing a melody within the wall of noise. But if I stopped concentrating, the slosh and pop of the static overtook the music again.

I moved toward the sound, past the gym and down a flight of steps past both of the locker room doors. It got louder to the point that I could feel the deeper gurgling notes rattling my chest. The melody grew clearer as I turned a corner toward the dead end hallway with just the door to an old boiler room ahead of me.

I turned the doorknob, and the sound stopped. Total silence again. I opened it slowly to reveal an emptiness, just nothing, like a pitch black lack of anything, on the other side.

Then I woke up.

◆　◆　◆

I always wind up getting to school pretty early and milling around in the hallway for a while. Today that went a little weird. It was still early enough that not very many people were there, but I ran into Beth by the Coke machine. She looked all excited.

"Come on," she said.

She grabbed my hand and had me follow her out into the parking lot to Nikki Turner's pale blue Ford Taurus. For whatever reason she had the keys to this girl's car, which was vacant. We climbed into the backseat and sat down. Beth jerked a pack of Virginia Slims and a purple lighter out of her purse and lit the skinniest cigarette I've ever seen.

"You smoke now?" I said.

She nodded.

"I don't know. I'm trying to get this whole eating thing under control and smoking makes me feel less stressed. Gives me something to do to take my mind off of everything."

People always suck at explaining why they have chosen to start smoking. I mean, once you're addicted, fine. That makes sense. But the weird rationalized excuses for choosing to get started are always nonsense. She went on:

"I've spent all of this time obsessed with control. My mom controlled me, and I wanted to control something of my own, so I developed this eating disorder. The whole world out there is made up of a bunch of people battling each other for control, but it never leads anywhere good. At some point you have to let it go, you know? You have to stop trying to control things and let them be."

Maybe I was annoyed by the smoking. Maybe it was something else. But I was in a pretty bad mood. I hammered out a fast drum beat on the rubbery blue door handle with my fingers.

"Well, smoking is a very attractive and desirable quality," I said.

Her mouth dropped open, and she laughed a little whispery chuckle. I think she thought I was just making a joke or something. Once her eyes searched mine and saw the complete lack of humor there, she swiveled her head away to look out the window.

"No, seriously," I said. "Sucking tar and chemicals into your body until your insides turn black? So sexy. That's what every guy wants."

She didn't move a muscle. Her head still faced away from me, completely still. Smoke spiraled off the end of the cigarette in her hand.

"You'll smell tremendous, too," I said. "The odor of your hair will always conjure my best memories of ashtrays and toothless people sitting on the stoops at a trailer park."

It felt weird. I'd never been so aggressive with her. On one hand, it felt good to finally assert myself, to stop being such a puss, and smoking really is dumb and unhealthy and everything, you know?

On the other hand, I don't know why I wanted to hurt her like this. I knew she was in trouble, and she needed help, but for some reason all this anger welled up in me, and I couldn't help myself. I'm sure I could've found a way to constructively criticize the smoking, but I don't think it was even about the smoking. Who the hell knows?

She unfolded the ashtray door and smooshed the cigarette into it.

"I'm sorry," she said. "You're right."

She leaned across the backseat and hugged me, resting her head on my shoulder. And part of me wanted to tell her I was sorry. Part of me felt like it was so pathetic for her to submit to my control so willingly after I treated her that way and wanted to stop it somehow. But I didn't do anything. I just hugged her back.

"I know you're only trying to help me," she said.

The cigarette still smoldered in the tray, so I picked up the butt and stamped it out for good.

◆ ◆ ◆

We always want more. I think we are coded for it, really. A team wins a championship, and they get right back out there to try to win another one. The richest corporations in the world only want one thing: More. Wal-mart built over 3000 new stores outside of the United States from 2005-2011. McDonald's builds a restaurant a day in China alone.

They have so much. They want more. They build more. They do more. More. More. More.

At some point, it starts to make sense. 'Cause you're never really done. You never reach a plateau of bliss and happiness where you just stop and relax. You want more, and you fight for more every day or you die. Retiring to a life of luxury is a death sentence. They talked about how a bunch of studies confirm that in my Psychology class. We aren't wired to be content. We aren't wired to coast. We are wired to fight. We are wired to endlessly work toward something. Anything. So the work never really ends, and there's only one motivator for work, truly: More.

Look at me, all I wanted was the girl, and once I kind of got her, I wasn't actually happy. I had complaints about the way she kissed me. And more than that, I just wasn't satisfied somehow. I want more. We always want more.

I knocked Troy down and stomped his ankle, but I'm not fulfilled. Now, I don't necessarily want to commit more violent acts against him or anything. I'm not satisfied is all. I solved that problem of Troy, but I want something else. I don't even know what it is that I want yet. Maybe it doesn't even matter what it is, so long as it's more.

Yep. More. Always.

I think maybe that is the meaning of life. Seriously.

CHAPTER 25

I WENT TO NICK'S HOUSE, and he was all drunk again. Just sitting by himself in the living room of his apartment chugging Budweisers. Ridiculous. His skin was all shiny and dark around his eyes, and he smelled pretty bad. He grunted, which I took as a hello.

"Hey, what's up?" I said. "Is Donnie at work?"

His eyes rolled. I guess that meant that Donnie was indeed assembling gorditas. (Maybe.) Even if that was pretty rude of Nick, he didn't have the hateful energy like he did the last time he was drunk. Really, he just seemed listless.

It didn't really make sense to me. He looked like he was on top of the world after we got that loaded jewelry box. What goes up must come down, though, I guess, and he'd crashed pretty hard. I'd never seen him like this.

"You doing alright?" I said.

He sighed heavily.

We sat in silence for a while before I finally turned on the TV and flipped through the channels. Donnie had rigged up the wiring so that they were leeching the neighbor's cable and got like every channel. Weirdly enough, I still couldn't find anything interesting to watch, though. I watched a few minutes of some guy working on a "pleasure garden" in his backyard, whatever the hell that means. Looked like a flower garden to me, but whatever.

All of a sudden, Nick leaned forward and sprayed vomit

fucking everywhere. It was insane. He made no attempt to stop himself or make a move toward the bathroom or anything. He just showered the floor and himself with beer foam and chunks of Wendy's chili.

"Jesus," I said.

Nick leaned back in his chair and closed his eyes.

◆ ◆ ◆

Weirdly enough, we talked about alcohol in Psychology today. So here's what I learned. We all have heard a bunch of times that drinking kills brain cells, right? Right. Well, what I didn't know was that the actual sensation of brain cells being damaged is what being drunk is. So basically people are killing their brain because it feels good. Weird, right?

So the booze gets in there and starts damaging the crap out of these things called dendrites, which are sort of like the stems at the end of brain cells that communicate from one cell to another. In other words, the damaged cells can no longer talk to each other. As people first get drunk, the inhibition of communication between these neurotransmitters and stuff give them a euphoric feeling. As the alcohol continues to take effect, though, it depresses the brain functions, which is why really drunk people seem to slow down. They slur their speech and their motor skills seem to deteriorate. Pretty soon they vomit all over goddamn everything. Shitty deal.

◆ ◆ ◆

"Come on," I said. "I'll clean this up, but you gotta change out of those clothes."

He didn't move until I yanked on his wrist to demand he get up. I laid paper towel over what seemed like gallons of vomit while he went and got a new shirt and everything. More and more fluid soaked up from the floor. I ran the roll of paper towel right down to the cardboard tube and had to resort to using a couple of beach towels as well — one with neon lobsters and crabs and stuff all over it, the other a full-size image of Hulk Hogan tearing his yellow Hulkamaniac shirt off. (I'm guessing that one is Donnie's.)

Nick came back out into the living room in fresh clothes and sat on the non-moist chair.

"Where's your wet shirt?" I asked.

"Meh," he said and shrugged.

Right. He leaned back again and seemed to be dozing off. I had to dig around in the dirty clothes on the floor of his room to find the offensive garment. I climbed down the steps to throw the beer and vomit soaked t-shirt and beach towels into the washing machine. My hands were all juicy by now. What a goddamn delight it is to babysit a drunk, eh?

Their basement was all cobwebby and seemed like the kind of basement that'd be full of spiders and cave crickets and such. Cardboard boxes lined the walls, and there were a couple shelves covered in various cables, cords, old WD-40 cans and stuff like that. The only thing that really stood out was a tattered old poster for the Wes Craven movie *The Hills Have Eyes* hanging over the dryer.

After I'd gotten the washer up and spinning, I noticed that one of the basement windows was all loose. It was fucked. Definitely not installed correctly. It was just kind of sitting there, the wooden frame not attached to the concrete foundation at all. The bottom half of the frame was leaning into the basement to the point that I thought it might fall and shatter everywhere, so I tried to push the whole unit into place.

Instead it kind of fell into my hands. I had an awkward hold of it, so I brought it down to my chest to adjust my grip when I realized that I could see under the back porch through the opening. That seemed odd. That they'd build the porch over this window, completely enclosing it. The soil under the porch was pitch black. And disturbed. It looked all lumpy and like parts of it had been dug up.

In the area just on the other side of the window sat one of several bulged spots in the Earth, and the ground there looked the most recently mussed.

I had a feeling I knew what it was.

I hoisted myself up so that my belly rested on the concrete, my legs still dangling into the basement. It smelled like roadkill under the porch, a penetrating sort of stench that I felt certain would cling to my hair and the fabric of my clothes for some time. I brushed the top layer of the dirt away and began grabbing handfuls to dig deeper. The smell got worse.

Eventually I exposed mannequin feet. It was weird. I knew they weren't really doll feet, of course. I knew it was human flesh, but I still saw them as mannequin feet for a moment before it really sank in. Ten toes with alternating pink and black nail polish, covered in chalky white powder that I assumed was lime. They'd shriveled some.

I froze. Jesus. It was what I expected when I saw the raised area in the dirt about the size of a body, but now that it was real, it was much more shocking. Disturbing.

Tammy was dead. And Nick had killed her. Her and who knows how many other people? Looking at the raised spots in this makeshift cemetery, he'd buried at least four of them down here.

I stared at the black mounds of soil, not able to blink or breathe or move at all. Nothing made sense. Everything I'd learned from him was somehow undone. I'd been learning from a monster. A serial killer.

Panic welled up in me. I smothered the feet with dirt as quickly as I could and hopped down into the basement. I shoved the window back into its spot, and it slammed into place with a bang that startled the crap out of me.

I turned to run up the stairs and get out of there. Nick stood at the top of the steps. He didn't seem so listless now. A wrinkle formed between his eyebrows. The hawk look.

"What the fuck are you doin' down there?" he said.

They were the first words he'd spoken to me that day, and he sounded so angry that I thought I was going to shit myself.

"I just threw the puke covered clothes into the washer. This window was hanging out, so I shoved it back in there. It's totally effed, by the way. The window, I mean. You should probably get the landlord to replace it."

He squinted. I'd basically nailed the lie, but he still seemed suspicious.

"Oh," I went on. "And you're welcome for me cleaning the hell up and all. But it's getting pretty late, so I'm going to go."

He didn't move, and I brushed right past him on the way out. I thought I carried myself right, though. I thought I fooled him.

Outside, however, I noticed that my hands were still caked

with black soil.

CHAPTER 26

I RAN STRAIGHT HOME AND gathered up supplies into a duffle bag: a flashlight, a hoodie, my brown cloth gloves, a blanket, this notebook and pen, a huge thing of beef jerky, a six-pack of chocolate pudding cups, a couple of Powerades, and several bottles of water. Thankfully, my mom was already in bed, so I didn't really have to worry about explaining why I was taking a bunch of food or where I was going with it at 11:30 pm. Not that I ever have to explain much to her, I guess.

So I can't decide if it was because I was scared of waking my mom or just plain scared of Nick, but I did all of this in the dark. The streetlights outside slanted bars of light through the windows that reflected off of the black and white ceramic tiles along the kitchen floor. I shuffled around in that half light and grabbed the things I needed. It was dark enough that the fridge light hurt my eyes and made me squint when I opened it.

Anyway, it's only been a couple of hours, but I barely even remember getting the stuff now. My head tingled the whole time, and my vision blurred and smeared along the edges. I think I was in shock. Maybe I still am to some degree, but my mind is a little clearer now, at least.

When the bag was full, I strode out into the dark. I wanted to be somewhere that Nick couldn't find me, so I figured I'd just walk around all night. Maybe find a decently secluded spot here or there to sit and think and write for a bit and then move on. I don't know. I felt like I had to keep moving. I still do, I guess. It feels like if I sit still too long, something will catch up with me, even if that doesn't really make sense.

The grass swished as I walked through it to get to the sidewalk. The manager for our apartment building is pretty lax about the landscaping, and the grass reached past my ankles.

It's hard to explain how messed up it all feels. It's like I've been building my identity on sand that just shifted beneath me and tore it all back down. Nick guided me, gave me confidence, believed in me, but was it all wrong? Can I keep some of it and throw the bad parts away? I mean, what am I supposed to think of it all? What am I supposed to do?

I walked down the railroad tracks and balanced on one of the rails like a tight rope for as long as I could without falling off. It was hard to get to twenty in a row at first, but I got the hang of it pretty quickly. Soon I could just keep going without falling off. My count of the paces got lost somewhere after I got to over 117 in a row.

A siren wailed in the distance.

I moved away from the lights of the city, and before long it was too dark to play the balance game without risking a fall. Black. I didn't want to trip over the beams either, so I walked in the gravel along the side of the tracks. It kind of hurt, to trod over all those points and hard edges.

The gravel crunched out a steady beat beneath me. When you walk a long distance, your thoughts start to take on the rhythm of your footsteps. A calm comes over you. Usually your mind goes as clear as water, but there's no clarity for me tonight. Only the pitch black nothing in all directions.

Wind whispered through the leaves in the treetops above me. It was too dark to actually see them, but the sound reminded me they were there. With the wind blowing, it was cool enough that I stopped for a second, pulled my hoodie out of the duffle bag and put it on.

I couldn't stop picturing the pink and black toenails shrouded in the earth under that back porch. I thought about who the other three people might be and shuddered. And it suddenly occurred to me that Nick had really only lived in that apartment for a few months now. Who knows how many others came before that?

A bell rang somewhere ahead of me, and red lights flashed where the train tracks crossed a road. A train was coming. I wandered down into the brush along the edge of the tracks and waited. Trees reached out knotty limbs that prodded at my neck and torso.

How could I not have known? It seems like if anyone in the universe should have known, it'd be me. I mean, I was the one that saw him strangle Tony Vasser all those years ago. I guess it's been so long that it didn't feel real anymore. It feels like a bad movie I watched a long time back.

The train chugged by very slowly. It was only a few boxcars long, and I couldn't imagine its small load being of any real significance. One time I watched a reality TV show where some real housewife of somewhere called every car in a train a caboose. None of the people she was talking to corrected her. Pretty dumb, but that's what sprang to my mind just then.

The smell of the decaying bodies still clung to my nostrils. The weirdest thing was how indistinguishable it was from a possum festering on the side of the road. I guess rotting meat all smells roughly the same. And that seemed weird, you know. How we're all just meat.

The train pulled around a bend and out of sight as I started down the tracks again. I was thinking about how the longer you're with someone, the more your brains start to wire the same way. I mean, you're sharing the same experiences, you know? Being exposed to the same sets of stimulus on a regular basis.

All of these things are etched into the circuitry of each of your minds. And you start to pick up on each other's speech patterns and thought patterns, too. You start knowing what they are going to say before they say it. I mean, Jesus, in certain circumstances, women in close quarters will even have their menstrual cycles synchronize if they spend enough time together.

So what did that mean about this time I've spent with Nick? Was it too much? Were we wired the same? Was he part of me now?

My mind kept running circles around these same ideas. And every new thought eventually trailed back into the same loop.

The violence of the crunch of the gravel beneath my feet made me realize that I was walking faster now. The moon glinted through gaps in the trees above to reveal the endless rocks stretched out in front of me like rows of teeth to stomp over and through.

As the reality of Tammie's death sank in, I began to sense the depth of it all. I think initially I couldn't really bear to confront it. I was in shock. And early on, I could only see it in terms of how it affected me directly and my situation, but now it was finally all becoming real.

I kicked up some gravel and a small chunk went down the

back of my shoe. It ground into my heel as I walked, and I stopped to pick it out.

I mean, I didn't even know Tammie that well, but I felt this empty space where she was supposed to be. I guess it must be something about the way our imaginations understand the world and the people we know. Before, when I thought she was in Ohio, she was gone, but I knew (incorrectly, of course) she was somewhere out there, and that was OK. Knowing now that she was actually gone — actually dead — felt different, though. And I'm talking about the feeling of it. My left brain knew she was gone — understood it to be factually accurate — but my right brain felt it. And it felt like my existence was a jigsaw puzzle with a gaping hole in it. Like something that was supposed to be there was just gone. The universe felt incomplete.

Waves of guilt crashed into me and tried their best to drag me under as I walked. I couldn't stop thinking about myself. I mean, I know that makes sense in many respects, but it didn't seem right to be having a mini-identity crisis — to be obsessing about myself, I mean — when someone else was dead.

To see someone else's death as merely something bad that has happened to you might be the most egocentric thing someone can do, but I guess it happens all the time. Maybe it has to. It's not like the dead person will get jealous or anything. It's not like paying attention to them instead would make anything better. Maybe that is what is so hard about it all. There's nothing useful to do with yourself in so many ways. Your mind just gropes along the edges of that empty space and can't make any sense of it, can't find any meaning in it, so you go back to thinking about yourself. It might be that's all you can do.

The weight of the duffle bag tugged at my hand and pulled one shoulder a little lower than the other. The bag bobbed at my side like a fishing lure on the water's surface, and it slapped into my thigh periodically. I peeled my hood down and ran my fingers through my hair.

You feel vulnerable out in the dark like this. Even after your eyes adjust and you get used to it, you feel alone. Empty. Doubt eats your soul right down to the core.

I came around a bend, and walls sloped up around me on each side of the tracks. A bridge. I had to clamber out of the rocks and walk on the planks. My footsteps suddenly sounded so different. Hollow. I thought about the scene in *Stand by Me* when the kids get out on the bridge, and the train comes barreling at them. They had to jump.

As I got to the middle of the bridge, I stopped. I turned and faced the wall, stepped toward it and ran my free hand along the cold steel. The duffle bag plopped down at my feet as my fingers released their grip. I climbed up onto the wall and stood and gazed over the edge of the bridge into the black water about half a football field below. The wind kicked up and blew my hood up onto my shoulder, so I swatted it back down. I could just faintly hear the water gurgling down there.

I dismounted the wall, scooped up the duffle bag and moved forward. It started to sprinkle. I held my free hand out to catch a few droplets and smeared the cool moisture between the tips of my fingers and thumb. Then I ran my moist fingers across my forehead, just above the brow. It felt good.

On the other side of the bridge, I trekked into a less wooded area, with cornfields on each side of me. No longer concealed by the branches, the swollen moon now joined me officially. It looked huge and not very high above the horizon, like my own weird sunrise of the night. With the moonlight providing better visibility, I continued to walk on the railroad ties. My feet needed a rest from trudging through the rock pile.

I came upon a stump shortly after that, and I decided to sit and write. I popped the foil top off of one of the pudding cups. Seconds later I realized that I hadn't packed any spoons. Shit. I tongued off the top layer of chocolate goo, smearing my chin in the process, but that only worked for about half of the cup. I ultimately had to resort to a series of finger dips.

Maybe it was the extra light or getting some food in my stomach, but I finally felt a little better now. I started working on a plan.

♦   ♦   ♦

Do you ever even think about these things? Do you care at all?

CHAPTER 27

THE WINDOW SLID OPEN WITHOUT a sound just like I
knew it would. (Of course, I don't know how I knew. I just did.
Maybe they opened this bathroom window to vent the room
often and forgot to lock it? Only one light switch, so there's not
a built-in vent. Anyway, that's my guess.)

I couldn't stop my thoughts from racing around everything
like that as I worked. My brain lurched into some hyperdrive
mania that I could not switch off. I wrote neurotic monologues
in my mind, endlessly commenting and speculating and
wondering about everything I encountered.

I ascended into the opening, my feet finding purchase on
the smooth burgundy bricks of the home's exterior. My arms
strained to pull my weight up onto the sill, and I poked my
head through the hole. (You always have to go face-first into
these things, I think. Always. There would be no more
hemming and hawing for me now, though. I plowed forward
once again.)

The lack of light surrounded me as I eased my torso over
the threshold and into the house. My hands reached out until
they found the carpet below. (The texture of the Berber felt
interesting through the brown cloth gloves. The tightly woven
bumps somehow reminded me of a head of raw cauliflower.
Cruciferous.)

(And I know what you're thinking, too. Carpet in the
bathroom? It's definitely not normal, but some people

apparently like it. And personally, I think these people aren't all that realistic about the sloshing and splattering that goes on in the bathroom on a consistent basis. Let's face it: A carpet in the bathroom is basically a sponge for bacteria and mold spores. Dr. Oz would be furious.)

I knelt between the toilet and frosted shower stall, the stench of a vanilla scented air freshener drifting around me. (Does anybody actually like the smell of these things, by the way? It doesn't eliminate foul odors. It doesn't really even cover them. Once it mingles with the poop smell, it's just a vanilla-ass fragrance. Nobody wins.) I unplugged the freshener and placed it in the trash gingerly enough to avoid making a sound.

I waited. I could hear a clock ticking loudly somewhere in the distance. The *tick-tock* sounded like a hammer banging at the silence in the house. That warm tingle came over me again. The feeling of adrenaline and electricity throbbing through my heart and streaming through my veins. This was being alive. Fucking terrifying, yes, but the biggest rush in the universe.

I flashed my light and turned right into the hallway, staying crouched. The cauliflower carpet stretched out in front of me, leading into the giant chamber that was the living room. Vaulted ceilings. Giant fireplace. The skylights let in enough moonlight for me to maneuver around the antique furniture (Seriously, it looked like something a goddamn king should sit on.) without my flashlight. I weaved my way left and started up the stairs.

The destination was so close now. Just a few steps away. I made sure to take it really slow on the stairway. My heart thumped in my chest. Sweat oozed from my forehead. I couldn't get over the idea of somehow blowing it at the last minute.

I pictured myself tripping and falling down the steps and bashing into glass cabinets, plates tumbling to the floor and crashing like cymbals. Pots and pans clanging into each other. Figurines of owls and cardinals taking suicidal plunges with glassy explosions of sound. But in real life I moved up another step and paused for a beat, moved up another step and paused for a beat.

I hesitated again at the top of the staircase and tried to take a deep breath as quietly as possible. I knew the sun would perk its head up very soon. It was a new day. I flashed my light for a second. To my left stood a white door with purple butterfly stickers plastered all over it. It was only opened a crack, so I shuffled over to it and slowly inched it open. It made the faintest tapping sound when it hit the door stop, but I don't think it was even as loud as the thunderous clicking of the clock that echoed through the house. Even so, I squatted in the doorway to let the sense of silence resettle itself over the room like a blanket.

My light revealed a twin sized bed in the far corner, with a lone figure in it. Long blond hair draped itself over the flowery pillowcase like a pile of spaghetti noodles spread over a plate. A pink bedspread with tiny white polka dots blanketed her. I moved in, stopping momentarily when my feet tangled in a pair of dirty jeans on the floor. My outstretched hand eventually felt the edge of the bed in front of me, and I stood from my crouched position to stand over it.

Birds sang outside the window, and gray light peeked in from the edges of the curtains. I needed to hurry.

I flashed my light and clasped my hand around the girl's

lips, shoving my face to her ear.

"Don't be afraid," I whispered.

My lips grazed her ear. She jerked, but I held her still.

"Beth, it's me," I said. "It's Jake."

I let her go and shined the light on my face so she could see me. She squirmed, but she didn't scream. This was good.

"What are you doing here?" she said. Her voice veered into that gravelly half whisper tone, which seemed so fucking loud just then. I could detect a lot of fear in it as well, which I had not anticipated.

I leaned in again. Her hair smelled really good like shampoo mixed with some kind of super soft suede.

"Beth, I think you might be in danger. I need you to come with me, and I need you to trust me."

It felt like a damn movie. She rubbed at her eyes.

"Well, let me get dressed," she said, whispering finally.

I turned my back and turned off my light.

◆　◆　◆

The garage door was still unlocked as I'd hoped. Beth and I made our way inside the empty house — the foreclosed one that Nick and I had mistakenly broken into. That seemed like forever ago. It looked different with the morning light streaming through the windows. Shiny wood floors sprawled everywhere. The rooms were all much smaller than I realized the first time, and each one was painted an interesting color. The living room was the color of eggnog, the master bedroom the color of butternut squash, the hall was the aforementioned Smurf blue from the paint cans in the closet, and the remaining

196

rooms were Carolina blue, cilantro, Prussian blue and lime green. Quite a mix. Seemed like a pleasant enough place, actually, but the lack of window coverings made me feel a little vulnerable upstairs, so after a quick look around, we went straight down into the basement.

We turned on our flashlights. Some light poured through the glass block windows, but it was still pretty dark down here. I realized that the basement walls matched the eggnog color from the living room. It was somehow calming. Maybe I was just delirious from lack of sleep, but the color reminded me of a room you would hang out with your grandparents in and eat ice cream or something.

"What is this place?" Beth said.

"Just an abandoned house. We'll be safe here."

She dusted off the top of a stack of cinder blocks lined against one wall and sat down. I dug in my duffle bag.

"You hungry?" I said.

"Not really," she said.

But I handed her a pudding cup anyway. We'd stopped at the grocery store on the way over, so we had spoons now and a few other things. Real metal silverware, too, though the handles were cheap red and black plastic. She scraped at the splotch of chocolate stuck to the foil lid.

"Alright," she said. "We're here. So explain."

I told her about finding Tammie's body in Nick's basement and everything. I kept it pretty brief. She didn't say anything when I was finished. She just sat her half-eaten pudding on the floor, and the weight of the spoon toppled it over, which startled her.

"Are you OK?" I said.

"Yeah," she said. "So you think... Why do you think I'm in danger?"

"You don't know Nick," I said. "He might do anything to try to hurt me now that I know. And I think he knows that going after you might be the best way to hurt me."

"So wait..." she said. "Why don't you go to the police?"

"I..." I said.

The truth was that I didn't have a good answer. The night had been so dark. Full of fear. Something about it just didn't seem right.

"I will," I said. "I'm just scared. And I wanted to make sure you were safe first."

I moved close to her.

"Come here," I said.

I hugged her, but her touch wasn't quite right. She felt far away. I think maybe she was pretty upset and all. She looked so nervous. But really she was OK now. I saved her.

It was weird to see her so upset when I was suddenly so relieved. I wanted to try to tell her something that would make her see it my way, but I didn't know how. Everything made sense to me now, though, here in the basement together. All of this was supposed to happen this way.

She leaned back against the wall and closed her eyes. I kind of figured she'd be tired like this. I yanked the blanket out of the duffle bag, managing to spill a lot of its contents onto the cement floor in the process. She took the blanket when I offered it to her and wrapped it around her shoulders. I leaned my back against the opposite wall and watched her for a time. I half expected the frown of concern etched in wrinkles on her face to fade as she drifted to sleep, but it didn't. Her breathing did slow down before long, and she was out.

My footsteps were precise and silent as I moved up the stairs. I glanced back to check on her every couple of steps, half expecting her to be staring back at me. She lay perfectly motionless, however. I closed the door behind me at the top of the steps, laced the padlock into the clasp on the door and locked it with a click.

CHAPTER 28

I PEERED THROUGH THE CRISS-CROSS of the lattice to see under the porch. Dunes and craters pocked the black soil there. Nick had already moved the bodies. I stayed on my knees a moment in the grass and tried to let it all sink in. That settled it. Nick knew that I knew. Not good. And yet I couldn't help but think about how much manual labor it would require to move four bodies by yourself, especially without anyone seeing you.

I stood and stretched, trying to work the soreness out of my back from the sleepless night of marching along the train tracks. I failed. Whatever action I took next would be hugely important, like life or death, but for some reason I was pretty relaxed. Calm wouldn't quite be the right word. This was a little colder than that, somehow. My mind was clear, in any case. I didn't even force any kind of decision. I let the ideas come to me. I let the impulses bubble up from my right brain, from somewhere in that cluster of primitive animal instincts. And the only thought that really came to me was to confront Nick.

I climbed the steps and pushed open the door. Nick sat in his usual spot in the living room. Alone. He looked utterly unfazed to see me.

"No school today, huh?" he said.

He was trimming his nails with the pocket knife again, and he had an open toolbox at his feet, which I gestured to.

"You working on something?" I said.

"Ah, it's nothing," he said. "Tightened up the wirin' on that light fixture in the bathroom that blinks. Or used to blink."

I nodded. I wondered how long it would go on like this, with the pleasantries and small talk flying back and forth. Nick folded the pocket knife up and tossed it into the toolbox. He leaned back in the chair and sighed.

"I tried my best," he said. "Tried to teach you everythin' I know."

He cupped the fingernail clippings in his palm and dumped them in the trash.

"I tried to toughen you up so you'd be ready to take on the damn world. 'Cause the world is so much worse than they're wantin' to pretend. And the people are so much more violent than they're wantin' to believe."

He stood up and brushed off his lap. I took a step back.

"Why'd you come here, Jake?"

I told him the truth.

"I'm not really sure."

He smiled, but he did not look happy.

"It was a mistake," he said.

He lunged at me, taking an angle that sort of cut off the doorway from me.

I rotated the opposite direction to get away, but now I was cornered. Shit. This guy was good at this.

He feinted to my left and lunged to my right, snaring me easily. His grip coiling around my upper arms. Jerking me toward him. Giving me one good shake.

His hands latched around my throat and squeezed. Cold fingers. Rough and hard as steel.

Thumbs depressing my Adam's apple. Shoving it straight back.

So much pressure on everything in my neck.

Crushing.

My eyes flushed with wet at the sheer force of his touch. The tears blurred my vision. Smeared it around so everything in the living room looked like it was behind warped glass.

I let my knees go limp without thinking about it and tumbled to the ground, getting in one last breath in the process as his hands momentarily loosened. He grunted and repositioned himself.

Nick's grip constricted once again. That bird look took shape in his eyes as they met mine. No real emotion for me. No regret. Nothing. Just aggression.

But I stared right back.

My hand flailed at the toolbox, fumbling over a few items before coming away with a Phillips screwdriver.

Nick adjusted his weight and tried to pin my arms under his knees, but I bucked and scooted myself back just enough to keep my arms free. Knocked him into a backward lean.

His being off balance gave me the only opening I would have. I knew this was it. This moment was everything. The only thing.

And the words repeated in my head:

Do or die.

Do or die.

Do or die.

I needed to do. So I did.

I jammed the screwdriver into Nick's neck all the way up to the handle.

His eyes went wide. Not scared, exactly. Shocked. Hurt, maybe.

I immediately pulled the screwdriver out, but the blood didn't gush freely like I was hoping it would. It trickled from the hole.

Nick's grip on my neck tightened, and his eyes got crazier than before somehow.

I took another swing with the screwdriver, but already my strength wasn't there. I missed and the tool got tangled in his shirt, tumbled out of my hand and skittered across the floor away from me.

You might typically be able to hold your breath longer than this, but I was fighting and panicking. The world started the fade to gray now. Black wouldn't be so far off.

Nick gurgled, and I saw blood on his teeth like a vampire's fangs in some shitty TV show. He suddenly released me and brought a hand to his throat.

I scrambled away, huddling into a corner on my back as breath wheezed and gasped its way back into my lungs.

He hacked a watery sounding cough that splashed blood into his hand. A lot of blood. His torso convulsed and tipped forward, and he caught himself with his hands on the floor, suddenly in pushup position with his head hanging a bit lower than his shoulders.

The blood poured out of his mouth and nose like a bathtub faucet turned up to full blast. Spurting. Gushing.

I cringed at the red spectacle, even if I'd caused it. Goosebumps plumped on my arms, my back. It just kept flowing out of him. Cascading. I couldn't believe it was real. It was the most disgusting thing I've ever seen.

The shallow pool of scarlet spread over the floor in all directions like a red flash flood overtaking a village. The word "gallons" popped into my head.

Within a few seconds, he plummeted to the floor face first with a disgustingly wet slap. He didn't move, but the blood kept spewing forth for longer than what seemed right.

I knew I must be covered in blood, so I rinsed off the best I could in the bathroom and changed into some of Nick's clothes. I found a plastic bag under the kitchen sink, and I threw the bloody screwdriver and clothes in it.

On my way out, I glanced at Nick's motionless body on the living room floor. Part of me expected him to be gone without a trace like Jason Vorhees in a *Friday the 13th* movie, but his corpse remained at rest. This was real life. Nick was dead.

CHAPTER 29

HOW DO THINGS GET SO crazy so quickly? You're just
going along, life is all normal, and—
   WHAM.
   Everything is different forever.
   Gigantic turning point. Impossible.

♦   ♦   ♦

I remember all of the action with intense clarity, but when I try
to remember how I felt about this, it's all blurry. I think maybe
I went crazy for a while. (Maybe I still am?)

♦   ♦   ♦

After disposing of the bloody evidence, I headed back to the
basement of the abandoned house to check on Beth. I brought a
pizza and orange soda and everything, but she still seemed
pretty upset. I saw her crumpled into the corner at the bottom
of the steps as soon as I opened the door.
   "I bet you're hungry," I said, gesturing to the pizza as I
trotted down toward her. The pizza was from Erbelli's, this
local place that wins all the awards and shit every year. They
put, like, garlic and cheese right in the crust, and when you
order extra sauce they smear a ladle full of marinara over the
top of the whole thing. It smelled fucking awesome.

She didn't rise to greet me or anything. She just stayed slumped there.

"You locked me down here," she said, her bottom lip quivering. Her eyes connected with mine for a brief instant, and then they flicked away in a flurry of rapid blinking.

"I was protecting you."

"You locked me in a strange basement for hours. This is not normal."

"Beth, I needed to know that you were safe. You don't understand. We're talking about a goddamn serial killer on the loose. A guy who kills girls and buries them under his porch, for Christ's sake."

"I want to go home."

"Oh, come on now. Let's eat this."

I tapped on the orange cardboard box. She didn't say anything. She started crying.

"Hey, enough of that," I said. "You're safe here. I'm protecting you."

I opened the pizza box, pulled out a slice of her favorite — no bullshit toppings, just extra cheese — and tried to hand it to her. She didn't move at all, so I leaned closer and pushed it right to her lips. To feed her, you know. She looked all scared, but she ate it. I fed her two pieces that way, but it was weird 'cause she just cried harder the whole time. Poor thing. I poured her a Dixie cup of Sunkist, and she drank some of that on her own at least.

After that I wolfed down the rest of the pizza, like six or whatever pieces, and polished off most of the two-liter of orange soda. I guess I was pretty hungry, you know?

When I looked over, Beth was wrapped in the blanket,

asleep again. The frown still creased her forehead and chin, which concerned me.

I wanted to tell her about Nick and everything that happened. To tell her she was really safe now, but I felt like if we left now, it'd just be messed up forever. We'd have to talk again first, and then I'd tell her. We could still straighten everything out.

They would have probably found Nick by now. I should be home. I crept up the stairs once again, padlocking the door behind me. I should point out that I did leave a stack of magazines for her to look through.

◆　◆　◆

I went home and pretended to do homework for a couple of hours. I propped a history book open on my desk and doodled in my notebook. I don't even know the real motivation for it. I just had this perverse desire to pretend everything was normal.

I heard the phone ring, and my mom answered it. She summoned me into the living room a few minutes later.

"Nick is dead. Murdered."

I didn't know if I should try to look sad or have some big reaction or anything. (I didn't. I don't think she noticed.)

"The cops think maybe it was payback for something that happened in jail. I guess it happens a lot more often than people think," she said.

In other words, the police aren't going to lose much sleep over a dead ex-con. I guess that's good for me.

The bad news was that everyone was already freaking out about a missing girl named Beth Horne. (Duh.) It's all on the radio and stuff. Authorities remain unclear about whether or not there is any link to the murder.

Yeah. Shit. Not great.

◆　◆　◆

I lay in bed awake most of the night, picturing Beth trapped down in that basement. It'd be so dark at night in there. Hope the flashlight batteries hold out for her. I was too paranoid to go back there this evening, though. It just felt like the whole town was on high alert or something.

Anyway, I twisted and turned in my bed. My arms felt wrong no matter what position I got into. And all I could think about was that I wished I had left her a bucket and some toilet paper, at least. I mean, there was a sump pit, I guess.

There was definitely no way out of that cellar, though. Those glass block windows were mortared directly to the concrete foundation and several inches thick, too. Even yelling would be pointless with the glass blocks in place. There'd be no gap or thin spots for the sound to travel through. The solid oak of the basement door might be considered the weakest point, but just barely. We're talking about one of those old, super heavy doors.

Yep. She would be staying put.

The lights and shadows danced over the walls in my room when cars passed outside my window. I could smell the rain outside and hear the wet when tires rolled over the asphalt. I kept getting too hot and ripping the blanket off, and then getting too cold and covering again. One of those nights.

I tried to come up with how all this would end. To imagine

it. How we could make the story make sense to everyone else, I mean. My mind concocted all kinds of lies, but I kept thinking it didn't really matter until I got everything straightened out with Beth. She was confused still.

I would go back after school tomorrow once everything else died down a little. It had been a while. I figured by now she'd get it. She at least had a couple pudding cups left, too. And some jerky, I think.

◆ ◆ ◆

I find myself undisturbed by all that has transpired. Calm, I guess. Does that seem wrong?

I wanted this. Didn't I? Needed it, I said. That feels like a long time ago now — a million goddamn years or so ago, give or take a hundred thousand.

When I lie in bed and close my eyes, I can still see Nick's body sprawled in that pool of blood. In my mind, it almost seems like so much blood that he's floating face down in it. A corpse drifting along in a red lake or river.

All of my life has led to this. This moment. This action. This set of circumstances.

I can see that now.

Still, I remain calm. Untouched by the shadows of the thing, I think, to a certain degree.

The violence. The blood. The death. These things seem shocking from afar, I'm certain, but they look different when you see them up close for yourself, when you participate in them. So different. They turn out so small, I think, once you're staring them in the face.

Yeah, I could resist the reality laid bare before me. Protest it. Get all emotional and frantic and everything, the way people do when confronted with death.

Or I could accept it. Deal with it. Figure out how best to move forward, how to get what I want. I guess that's what makes sense to me, the only thing that makes any sense at all.

The sheets go warm against me as I sprawl here in the dark. I can't help but miss the cool of them in a way, that soft chilly touch that made my skin pull taut.

I keep lying down for a few minutes at a stretch. Staring up at the ceiling. Telling myself that I'm done writing for now and that I need to sleep.

Instead I sit up again. Flick on the flashlight. Arm myself with this pen to scratch out more words. The stream of thoughts never fully stops, I guess, and the pen wants to keep up.

I close my eyes and see him again. Prone. Face mashed down in the red. Hard to believe that a powerful creature like Nick could be cut down, could be stilled like this. That's the one part that's somewhat disturbing, I guess. The way the light can just cut the fuck out to black for any of us in a second. No warning. No take backs. No matter how tough you are.

But then I think about it a little more, and I wonder what disturbs me more. That someone as strong as Nick can get taken out? Or that I was the one powerful enough to do the deed.

Me. I did this. I controlled the situation. Stood up for myself. Protected myself. With nothing more than my mind and my hands, I separated life and death.

All the things the lessons were supposed to teach me? They

did.

Funny how life works.

I wanted this. The lessons. The change. The shift in myself, in my mindset, in my life. Needed it, I told myself.

Maybe I did.

CHAPTER 30

SCHOOL DRAGGED ON FOREVER. I couldn't really pay attention to anything. My eyes drifted to the clock over and over and watched it not move. I noticed that the minute hand on some of these ancient clocks actually moves slightly backward for the first thirty seconds of each minute and then gets caught up down the stretch and pushes forward to the next minute right on time. At first, that kind of fucked with me. When I watched the damn minute hand move backward, you know. I thought I was losing it.

I got the worst headache in the afternoon. Couldn't wait to get home to take some ibuprofen. That works best for me for some reason. Better than aspirin, acetaminophen and naproxen and all of that, I mean. (Whenever I see a commercial for Bayer Aspirin, I think it sounds like they're saying "bare ass burn" for a second. True story.)

It's weird to sit in a classroom full of people and feel apart from all of them. To watch their faces, the same look in all their eyes, all so occupied in their own worlds that they don't even notice someone observing them. To watch all their pens and pencils flutter in unison. To watch their brows furrow in concentration. And what for? All of that effort for what? It all seems so meaningless somehow.

I felt like a spider, watching and waiting. Patient. But ready.

◆　◆　◆

I brought lots of supplies this time. Better safe than sorry, right? It's weird, actually. Did you realize they have quite a selection of groceries and everything at the hardware store now? Pretty ridiculous, but also pretty convenient in this case. I was able to toss everything straight into a bucket and not look like I was toting around a bunch of bags of stuff.

Like I said, though, I stocked up. I got a 5-gallon bucket, toilet paper, batteries, candles, peanut butter and jelly, a loaf of bread, some fruit snacks that are loaded with vitamins, and a bag of Harvest Cheddar Sun Chips. (I think Beth likes those. Not sure.) They had these super cheap off-brand sports drinks that I decided to try, too. (You know me. I'm a sucker for a great beverage at a great price.)

As I advanced into the basement, I started to get a sick feeling. What if she was hurt or something? My mind sketched a portrait of her dead body slumped against the cinder blocks, her lips drawn back, and her tongue lolling out the side of her gaping mouth like a St. Bernard's. The skin on her face graying like ash and crumbling away. (That made a fragment of a lyric from some shitty song pop into my head: "slip sliding away." No idea.)

She was fine, though. (Physically, at least.) She'd moved to the farthest corner from the steps, the blanket slung over her shoulders like a cape.

"Do you like Sun Chips?" I said. "I couldn't remember."

She didn't say a word. She didn't even look at me. Her hand moved to her face and scratched under her jaw.

"These are..." I said. I had to check the bag. "These are harvest cheddar flavored. I hope that's the right kind."

She blinked, but her stare remained fastened to the wall.

The silent treatment, eh? Honestly, I wasn't sure what she was trying to accomplish with this tactic.

I smeared peanut butter and jelly on a couple of slices of bread. I figured she'd be hungry at least, right? When I brought the sandwich to her, though, she swiveled away from me. Her shoulders squared to the corner now, so I could barely see her face at all.

I retreated and left the sandwich on a paper plate atop the overturned bucket. I put a pack of fruit snacks and a handful of Sun Chips on the plate with it like a real lunch. Like this was just a picnic or something.

"Well, I can see that you're not in the mood to talk, so I'll get out of here," I said.

I saw her flinch out of the corner of my eye, but I decided not to look at her directly. I ascended the steps and stopped for a second at the top.

"Just try to keep in mind that I'm keeping you safe from a goddamn serial killer once in a while, would you?"

I moved through the door and slammed it behind me. Next I opened and closed the door leading outside as though I'd gone through it and held still just outside the basement door.

The scuffing and scraping of her scrambling across the basement was followed by the pound of her feet moving up the steps. The doorknob twisted to no avail, and she rattled the door the best she could, which was not all that much. The padlock quivered but just barely.

"Are you there?" she said, which kind of startled me. She yelled the next time. "Are you there?!"

She shook the knob again.

"Come back," she said. Her voice was soft now. "I'm sorry."

I heard a single thud on the door, the sound of her forehead resting against it in frustration, I think, and then all was quiet.

I waited. In a weird way I wanted to laugh, like one of those super serious moments that you're absolutely not supposed to laugh, you know? Like church or a funeral or something? I bit my lip, though, and held it together.

Slow footsteps paced back down to the cellar, and I heard the scrape of the bucket moving a moment later as well. Good. She was eating her lunch.

◆　◆　◆

I forgot to mention — the sports drink was actually really good. I should specify: the orange flavor was good, at least. I went for orange and blue. I think it was a good choice. I feel like the lemon-lime is always shitty no matter what brand, you know? And the red is OK, but it's always a hair too sweet for my tastes. (I don't even get into all that fierce melon type shit, so don't ask.)

Anyway, I haven't tried the blue yet, but I will let you know.

◆　◆　◆

I waited upstairs for a good twenty minutes before I finally faked the sound of myself returning and headed back down. She was sitting on the cinder blocks, the mostly empty plate resting on her lap. She stared up at me.

"I'm glad you're eating," I said. "So was I right about those Sun Chips or what?"

"Yes," she said. "Thank you."

We just looked at each other for a long moment. She smiled, but there was something oddly timid about it, I thought. She still didn't quite seem like herself.

"Where'd you go?" she said.

"What do you mean?" I said.

"When you left and came back just now," she said.

"Oh. I walked around the block, you know," I said. "Trying to clear my head. It's frustrating. This is all so confusing."

I pawed at my chin before continuing, I guess for dramatic effect.

"But I'm sure you know that better than anyone."

She looked down.

"Yeah," she said. "I guess so."

Silence fell upon us again, but it wasn't so unpleasant anymore. (For me, at least, but I think for her, too.)

"So how long do you think I'll need to stay here?" she said.

God. I couldn't help but smile, but I coughed to cover it up real fast.

"Not long," I said. "Probably only a couple more days at the most."

"Do my parents even know where I am?" she said.

I shook my head.

"I couldn't risk it," I said. "Your safety is the only thing that matters to me now."

I actually thought about saying 'Your safety is of paramount importance,' like in a movie or something, but it sounded a little too ridiculous in my mind. Anyway, I walked over to her and put my arms out, and she stood to hug me. Finally.

I sat down on the floor next to the cinder blocks, and she crawled down to lay across my lap. The blanket bunched around her neck. I raked my fingers back and forth through her hair, and we talked for a long time after that.

I don't think I've ever been so happy as I was to win her back like I did. A brightness spread through my whole body.

She talked about her dreams, I guess since she'd been sleeping so much. She dreamed that we were at some party and she couldn't find me, and all of the people were drunk and couldn't talk right. They kept saying that I'd "gone thither." And she had dreams of a black shape on top of her, pinning her down, and she couldn't move or breathe. And one where she was alone and lost in a gigantic building that never ended. She ran down hallways and up and down stairs into never-ending chambers and corridors.

"So was I right about those damn Sun Chips or what?" I said. "The harvest cheddar?"

"Yeah," she said. She sounded sleepy again.

"Good."

♦ ♦ ♦

Beth nibbled a microscopic piece off the corner of a Sun Chip. She was finally talking like things were normal.

"One of the craziest things you realize when you're growing up is how your parents don't really give a shit about you," she said.

"Yeah," I said.

The way she held the chip to her mouth and took these tiny bites off it reminded me of the way a squirrel eats.

Nibble nibble nibble.

Stop.

Nibble nibble nibble.

Stop.

"I mean, they care that you're like... alive, but the actual details don't matter. The things that make you who you are, they don't care about those things. They want you to be a certain way, so they'll just pick and choose what things they accept and what they don't."

The nibbling continued as she spoke.

"Like last spring, my mom took me shopping for summer clothes, and she kept trying to pick out bathing suits for me. I haven't worn a bathing suit or gone swimming in about three years, but she has no idea, I guess. How can you be my mom and not notice that? How can she just forget that every time we go to the lake, I don't wear a bathing suit? I don't get in the water."

She shook her head.

"And even the bathing suits she was picking out weren't me at all. They had like ruffles around the hips. The kind of thing I wore when I was two. It's like my whole existence is in her imagination. She just makes things however she wants in her head."

Her eyes rolled up to the ceiling, and she shrugged.

"I finally just let her pick one so we could be done with it. Some hideous monokini thing that was brown with pink and white and green flowers. And of course I never wore it and never will. But she won't remember. Or she'll choose not to. Next time it will be the same thing all over again."

She had managed to finish the single Sun Chip, and she brushed the neon orange cheese powder off her fingers.

I nodded. I didn't know what the hell a monokini was, but I

didn't think it mattered.

"I know exactly what you mean," I said. "My mom still buys me tighty-whitey underwear, despite the fact that I've exclusively worn boxers since I was ten. And they're always two sizes too small."

Beth stared at the far wall, her eyes unfocused. She shook her head slowly.

"It's like they're not even paying attention."

◆　◆　◆

She turned to look up at me, her eyes wide. Scared.

"Don't leave me," she said. "You can't leave anymore. You have to stay with me tonight."

"OK," I said. Of course, this was not happening. I couldn't risk staying out all night again now that she was known to be missing. People might link those things. (And by "people" I mean the kind with guns and badges and such.)

Anyway, she narrowed her eyes at me.

"Do you promise?" she said.

"Yeah. Jesus. I promise, alright?"

She turned away again.

"It's too scary at night."

I pinned her shoulders against my thighs so she wouldn't fall over as I leaned forward to grab one of the blue sports drinks and cracked it open. Dude. Even better than the orange kind. For real. It's fucking delicious.

"Try this," I said, thrusting the blue drink at her.

She propped herself up with her elbow and took a drink. Her expression didn't look all that impressed, though I'm not sure what I expected, to be honest.

"Pretty good," she said.

It was weird. This lack of enthusiasm suddenly meant the world to me. It undid the kinship I felt earlier when we were talking about our families. This feeling came over me where I kind of knew for sure that no matter what the hell you ever do, you're alone. And other people might care some, they might even want to care all the way, but they ultimately never care that much. They only want to find their own things to be excited about.

Like I found this sports drink, and I was feeling awesome, but she doesn't care, you know? She has her own things to worry about. Sure, it's just a dumb drink. It probably sounds ridiculous, but it made everything click for me somehow.

And I thought about this thing I've been writing. Would she care? Probably not. She might be curious enough to read it, but that'd be about it. Only if she could consume it and somehow make it a piece of her identity would she really care, I think. Just like everyone else.

In the end, we're all alone. We're always separate.

I suddenly wondered if Beth had made herself vomit down here, but I guess I'd probably smell that, right? I mean, it couldn't just disappear. It's not like I could really ask her in any case.

But then I thought about the poop and pee issue. That wouldn't spontaneously vanish either, of course, but harvest cheddar was the only odor in the room.

"So where have you been," I said, pausing to search for the right words, "you know, going to the bathroom?"

She sat up.

"Do you have to go?" she said.

"Oh. Yeah," I said.

(Like it wasn't merely morbid curiosity.)

"Well, number one is in that utility sink around the corner."

She pointed to a paint-smeared white sink across the room.

"You just run a little water after," she said.

"Wait. The water is on?"

"Yep."

"Weird."

"For number two, you gotta squat over the sump pit, though," she said. "But, in either case, if you just pull up on that bar, it triggers the sump pump and flushes it all away. Or maybe not all, I guess, but, you know, a lot of it."

I thought about it for a second.

"So the water *and* the electricity are on?"

She shook her head.

"For some reason none of the lights work, but the sump pump does."

That made sense, I supposed. Leaving the sump pump on would be a safety measure against flooding or etc.

I picked myself up and headed to the sink. May as well take a leak in here for the novelty of it all, I figured.

◆　◆　◆

I woke up from a half-sleep in the basement and realized it was dark outside. My back hurt from lying on the hard concrete. Beth had turned both flashlights on and nestled them in her shoes to angle them up and sort of light up our area of the room as well as possible without the beams shining directly in our faces. I yawned and stretched.

"I like the idea of *A Nightmare on Elm Street* more than I actually like the movie," she said.

Fuck. I needed to find a way out of here, and she was really going off on horror movies.

"What you do mean?" I said.

"The idea of some mysterious supernatural entity being able to attack you through your dreams? That's actually scary."

"Yeah."

"The concept is awesome, and the first movie isn't bad, but they get so much worse."

"Well, yeah."

"But I also like that Freddy Krueger is a little more particular, too. Jason Vorhees and Michael Myers are just psychos wearing masks. So you can't see their faces, and then on top of that, they barely have any motivation. Freddy Krueger is all creepy and burned and was murdered. And he was a bad guy before he got murdered. Scarier."

"You think so?"

"Well, I mean, yeah. Freddy toys with his victims. He prolongs the chase part because he is sadistic. The thrill is his motivation, and we can see that on his face."

"So basically Freddy does a fifteen-minute comedy routine complete with one-liners before he actually kills somebody, and that is superior," I said.

She laughed.

"Well in the later movies it gets ridiculous, yeah. Anyway, Jason chops down his victims four at a time with a machete after they have sex or do drugs or something. But why? For enjoyment? Is he some kind of crazed moralist? Or is it solely revenge for the way he was mistreated or whatever by the camp counselors? We don't see his face, and he doesn't speak, so we can't really say."

I listened to the silence of a lull in the conversation. I could not imagine how the hell I would ever get out of here without her freaking out.

"In the end," she said, "the idea of Freddy is a lot scarier than the actual figure on screen, though. Seeing his picture with the burned face and the glove and everything as a kid and having it left to my imagination was terrifying."

Jesus. I thought we were done with Freddy, for Christ's sake. It's just like the movies. He resurrects for another damn sequel.

I stood up and wiped at the dust clinging to my pants.

"Look, I've got to go," I said. "I'm sorry."

Her face twisted up into a mask of evil, not so unlike Freddy's, to be honest, and she sighed one of those aggressive heaves of a sigh.

"You promised," she said.

I shrugged, palms upturned, and her bottom lip dropped open to reveal clenched teeth. She jumped up into a crouched stance like a linebacker before the snap. Her feet pivoted to position her body between me and the door.

"What's this all about?" I said.

She didn't say anything, but her arms splayed out to her sides. They danced back and forth there like charmed snakes, waiting for me to make a move. I knew then, without a doubt, that any progress we made this afternoon was long gone. Flushed away like the turds in the sump pit.

Tim McBain & L.T. Vargus

"This is all for your safety, remember?" I said.

"No," she said, her mouth still clenched. "No, you don't understand. If you leave me here again, I will never forgive you. Ever."

I stepped forward. She dove, splaying out flat to grasp after my ankles. I juked and kicked my feet up, but she got a piece of my pants with her claws and the rest of her sort of latched around my leg. It reminded me of a bee's legs wrapping around your finger just before it stings you.

"Let go," I said.

I strained to step free from her grip. My calf bulged. Her knuckles whitened. I paused for a second and struggled against her again, trying to catch her off guard. Not a chance. I let up.

"All right," I said. "I'll stay. Just let go of my foot already."

"You're lying," she said.

She hugged herself against me harder, blonde hair swirling over her face.

"I'll never let go."

"Fine."

I bent over at the waist, resting my hands on my knees. Let her hold on, right? Let her wear herself down, gripping all tight like that. Yep. Go for it, dude. No sweat off my back. I'd just wait her out.

I thought about that feeling you get when your team is losing. That terrible, helpless sensation like everything in the universe transpires out of your control. The opponent keeps your tribe on the defensive. Keeps attacking some weakness that usually isn't there, but today it is, and you can't fix it. Your will power seeps away like air gushing from a popped tire. It feels like you've been punched in the gut, and you'll never win again. Never have control again. And always, the clock ticks down toward zero.

People watch sports 'cause it simulates life and death, especially in any kind of playoff scenario. Winning is survival. Losing is death. We all survive and die vicariously through teams or boxers or poker players or whatever.

But it was weird, 'cause I knew I wasn't going to lose this time. Eventually she would let go. She'd fall asleep. She'd lose focus for just a second. She'd get hungry. She'd have to go to the bathroom. She'd scratch some itch that she could no longer ignore. Whatever the case might be, she would let go, and I would go home.

Still, I had that feeling. Losing. Powerlessness. Death. Something wild thrashed out of my control, and beat me down, and laughed in my face all the while.

Silence smothered us. Tranquility taunted us. I could see her chest throb when she breathed, but otherwise there was no movement. No noise. Nothing.

I ripped my leg free. I guess her mind had wandered after all.

"No!" she screamed.

She scrambled to try to get to her feet, and I gave her a shove, almost a stiff arm, while she was off balance. She staggered into one of those running-slashing-falling-forward maneuvers. That gave me just enough space to race to the top of the stairs and get the door closed behind me.

"No!"

She hurled herself at the door, thumping on it again and again. She screamed all the while, mostly wordless, though she threw in some profanities here and there. Her voice was all raw and shrill. There was something almost demonic about it.

I waited for a long time there, listening to her hysterics. I don't really know why. That feeling of losing really swelled in my belly then, though I was still clueless as to why. I'd seemingly won in the short term, but everything had just careened out of my control again. I could feel it all around me. The world turned against me somehow, with gleeful cruelty, like a thousand kicks in the sack.

It fucking hurt.

CHAPTER 31

ONCE AGAIN, I DIDN'T SLEEP so much as flail about that night. Kicking, twisting, swinging my arms, I brawled with the blanket and stomped on the sheets. My head-butted the pillow. My mouth tasted like that wet dog smell mixed with pond scum. I could hear my heartbeat like someone pounding out a never-ending drum fill on my eardrum.

I kept imagining a realtor coming to do some kind of walk-through at the vacant house early the next morning. I pictured an older woman with long dark hair and huge square glasses. She sported a pink and purple Cosby sweater and khakis and thumbed through a huge ring of keys before letting herself in.

Leaflets were laid out on countertops.

Febreeze spritzed everywhere.

She sliced open one of those Tollhouse loaf tube things of premade cookie dough and started cutting it up onto a metal cookie sheet. To give the place that smell of cookies baking, you know?

And then Beth started moaning from the basement and rattling chains like she was some animal caged down there. Like Frankenstein's monster or something. And the realtor's mouth popped open, and she dropped the cookie dough tube, which slapped and half-flattened on the kitchen floor. And the knife skittered over the cookie tray and onto the counter.

I coiled the sheet into knots around my knees. The blanket crept up over my shoulders, and I bashed it back down. I didn't fluff the pillow so much as pummel that shit.

I really hadn't had a decent night's sleep in several days now. (Since the whole Nick thing. Jesus. I'd barely even thought of that all day. And I won't start now. I will leave it here in the parenthetical world and just move on. It's too much.)

The warmth crawled over my face then. The adrenaline and excitement and fear of it all. I knew I wouldn't sleep, but I lay there in the dark anyway. I guess I wriggled more than I lay, but you get the point.

The words "still life" popped into my head, like the art of inanimate objects. Paintings of bowls of fruit and shit, you know. Maybe the words came to me because I couldn't keep still. I don't know. It's weird how that name, still life, is more interesting than the art itself in some ways.

Loads of people lead a still life, I think. The stillest life of all. All the people that work the forty-hour-a-week office jobs and factory jobs and retail jobs and all that. The years of their life just melting away.

I could be wrong. I don't claim to know everything. But from a distance I see no purpose in it. No meaning. No growth.

They cart themselves to and from work so they can buy new furniture and bigger TVs. What drives them to it? Don't they ever wonder what for? Can't they feel the emptiness of it all? Weren't we made to be part of something bigger somehow? Something that actually matters.

But I also knew I could never have a still life now, even if I wanted it. I'd crossed some line somewhere, some permanent threshold, and that was over for me.

Maybe none of it matters anyway. Isn't that what Nick was

trying to say, really? That there is no meaning in any of it no matter what.

All the things that drive our desires. The things we think we want coming from somewhere deep in a hole in our right brain that we can never peer into.

So we ceaselessly struggle against each other. We clash. We crash. We collide. We lie and cheat and steal. And kill.

But it's all in some false hope. Because there's nothing there.

Our left brain tries to etch order into the chaos. It believes until the very end that our right brain is telling us these things for a purpose, a reason, that there's a pot of gold at the end of the goddamn rainbow. But there's not. Deep down, you know there's not.

There's only the pitch black nothing.

◆　◆　◆

Beth leaned against the wall under one of the windows, standing. Fractured sunlight curled down onto her through the glass blocks and fluttered over her face in a way that made it look like she was under water.

Her eyes were open too wide somehow. They tracked me across the room, but otherwise she stood motionless. I couldn't get a read on her expression. I planted my feet a couple yards short of her, and we looked at each other.

"You must really get off on all of this, huh?" she said. "Keeping a girl trapped in the basement like a grasshopper in an old pickle jar with breathing holes stabbed in the lid."

I didn't say anything.

"Is that the only way you could actually get a girl, do you think? Kidnapping and imprisoning her?"

"No."

"Oh, please. You always knew that this was never going to happen. Not really."

She undulated her hands between us in a way that signified that by *this* she meant her and I being together romantically.

My eyes traced a steel beam across the ceiling.

"But you're the one who kissed me," I said.

"For fuck's sake! I felt sorry for you. And I was bored. Look, Jake, you are a nice guy, mostly. You really are, and you were always a good friend to me, but you're just not..."

She trailed off, apparently unable to find the words to properly capture my inadequacy as a man. I filled in the blank a thousand ways in my mind.

"This has gone on way too long, and you know it. You've gotta let me out of here. You know it's the right thing to do. You know it's the only thing to do now. This entire situation is ridiculous. It's over. Let's go home."

The whole world faded out. My consciousness filtered down to the sound of my heart beating again, just like it did squatting in some strange house in the middle of the night. I think she kept talking. Kept pleading her case. But I only heard the bang of that misshapen muscle in my chest pumping blood all through me.

And I guess I don't really remember how it started. I just remember feeling the strength in my hands. Impossible strength that squeezed at Beth's throat.

Closed it.

Crushed it.

I felt all those tubes collapse under the pressure of my grip. It felt good.

And I remember how scared she looked. Her eyes huge and blue and wet with fear.

Her mouth sprang open, and her tongue flapped about like it could somehow get out of the way and she'd be able to breathe again or something.

And it was funny 'cause she barely even fought me. Her fingers dug at my arms a little bit, but she didn't even break the skin. She didn't reach for my face. She didn't kick at me. Nothing. She just lay down to die like a perfect victim.

She let me do it. She was so soft.

I mean, she squirmed. That's about the best you could say for her efforts. She squirmed. Pretty pathetic.

My heart hammered in my ears the whole time. I could hear the sound of my own survival while I took hers away. And it felt that final, too, even before it was over.

Like I was setting the whole world on fire and burning it to the ground.

I could feel her fear like it was vibrating off of her. Some wave in the air that penetrated my skin. And I knew that in some way Beth and I would be together forever now. In this basement. In this final embrace. Forever.

Drool cascaded from the corners of her lips like a mouth-breathing hound dog with those two thick strings of spit hanging down.

Her face went all splotchy and darkened into the progression of colors, just like Tony Vasser's outside of Dairy Queen all those years ago. It was weird 'cause I remember thinking how nice her skin looked just then. The texture of it, I mean. All smooth and creamy like the surface of a glass of milk.

Her color was fading from purple to blue when she passed out, but I knew I wasn't done. Not yet. I squeezed the fuck out of her neck. I kept expecting my hands to cramp up, you know, but they never did. I'm pretty sure I could have choked her forever.

Her face was all gray now like someone smeared charcoal all over it. It didn't look real. It just seemed like some special effects sequence in a not so scary horror movie. The ones that just make you laugh the whole time.

It wasn't until I finally let go and tried to uncurl my fingers that I felt the pain in them. The stiffness. Beth's body did a free fall to the floor like a dummy and something kind of crunched on impact. The back of her head maybe. I'm not really sure.

I stood over the corpse and massaged at my hands, straightening my fingers out over and over. Stretching them. My mind was weirdly clear. Not any kind of religious or philosophical clarity, I mean. Just clear of thoughts. Empty. Blank.

I looked her over. Even as fucked up as she looked, all gray like that, I kind of expected her to get up. Like part of my imagination couldn't reconcile the idea that a few minutes ago she was alive and now she was dead. Forever. It didn't seem really possible. Like whatever magic electrical juice flowing in her nervous system that made her alive before was just gone and would never come back. Physically, she was identical. Same body. Same organs. Same brain. But the juice was just gone for good.

I grabbed the wrists and dragged the body over to the sump pit and scooted it into the water. It flopped in head first, and the trunk of the body seemed to kind of hesitate over the hole before it fell and yanked the limp legs behind it in a weird way that reminded me of Wile E. Coyote holding up a sign before he falls off of a cliff. I remember reading that once a body is immersed in water, it's like a million times harder to get any evidence or whatever off of it. It messes up the body temperature, too, for determining the time of death.

Anyway, the pit was only like four feet deep so the socked feet dangled out of the top. It looked like a joke. Like those fake arms and feet people have sticking out of the trunk of their minivans and stuff.

I tilted my head into the sink and splashed some water on my face. I didn't dry it off. I just rested my weight on the lip of the sink and let the moisture drip away. Wetness clung to my jaw and tried its best to hold on, but the droplets formed and fell. Slowly, but I was patient. My face was all flushed, so the cool water felt nice. The drips eventually stopped, but I stayed there, elbows rested on the sink's edge.

Eventually I realized that I was lingering there. That part of me didn't want to leave yet. Isn't that weird?

But I also knew, of course, that leaving would be for the best. I gathered up my things and headed up the stairs. I peeled the padlock out of the clasp and shoved it in my pocket. Again, I hesitated. I looked around the kitchen for a second, looked at the empty spots where clumps of dust and hair had replaced the stove and fridge.

I walked out into the garage and observed its emptiness as well. As my feet shuffled near the door, they paused for another beat. My sleeve covered hand hung a moment just short of the doorknob. I have no clue what I might have been waiting for.

Nothing happened, of course.

I pushed open the door and stepped away from the building.

That's when I woke up.

CHAPTER 32

I SPRANG FROM THE BED and threw on the dirty jeans and t-shirt from the day before without thinking. I guess they were the closest garments, maybe. My mind was going a million miles a minute about non-hygiene and fashion related topics just then.

The dream rattled me. Things I had never seen about myself came clearer now. Though I didn't fully know what to make of it, it all made more sense than ever in its own way.

Remember all of that stuff I said about the bullies being obsessed with control and how I wasn't like that? Yeah. I'm full of shit. I needed to see Beth immediately.

♦ ♦ ♦

"When you're a kid, you look for order in the universe. That's how you learn everything. Like, when I was a toddler one time I fell asleep on the couch in the afternoon. And when I woke up a couple hours later, it was dark out, right?" I said.

She nodded and leaned back so the crown of her head rested against the cinder block wall.

"I remember thinking that must mean that if you go to sleep in the living room, you wake up at night. 'Cause I knew that whenever I went to sleep in my bedroom, I woke up in the morning. I thought I controlled the whole day turning to night and vice versa thing based on where I slept. I looked for order

235

— a pattern in what little data I had — to try to understand how it worked, and that's what I came up with."

"I get it," she said.

I scratched my chin.

"Nick gave me… He was trying to teach me. He had me shoplift and get drunk and help him break into houses and stuff. He was trying to teach me how the world really works, or the order he sees in it, at least."

I sighed, trying to think of the best way to explain it.

"He talked about how all these corporations lie and cheat and steal to get what they want. 'Cause they filter all of the meaning out of the world until all that's left is profit. Like the cigarette companies were literally killing their customers and lying about it all those years 'cause the only thing that's real to them is the money. Right and wrong no longer exist. The money in the bank account is the only reality. So Nick looked at all of that together, and he thought it meant that there's no real meaning in anything. Like everything we're taught is a big lie."

I swallowed and continued.

"He said the world operates in chaos, you know? No good. No bad. No morality. It's all just a sequence of events without meaning. We're just animals that are here for a short while, and seeing it as anything beyond that is just mushy stuff or delusion."

Shrugging, I picked at a dried fleck of cafeteria marinara on my jeans.

"So I looked at all of that, too. And I tried to find my own order in it, I guess. I started having all of these dreams. About you, mostly."

Her lips moved slightly, but I couldn't read her expression.

"If you take the meaning out of the world, all that's left is controlling each other. Even a sociopath with no empathy at all still gets the animal urge to establish a place in the pecking order. Like bullies at school, you know? If you can't actually connect with other people, it just leaves controlling people, asserting your will, getting what you want out of them. Winning. Like other people are just another thing to consume. We are driven to do it way beyond what makes any damn sense."

I played with the strings on my hoodie.

"And I didn't realize it right away, but these dreams were all about controlling you. At first, it's like I was saving you. Like we'd be surrounded by zombies, and I would rescue you and take you some place safe. And that meant you needed me, like I could sort of require you to love me that way, you know?"

My lips felt dry and chapped. I ran my tongue over them.

"And then over time, it got weirder, like you were more and more scared of me, and everything was all confused, and it was more like I was directly controlling you against your will. Taking you somewhere. And then…"

I told her about the last dream. In detail. Her shoulders looked tense and she blinked a lot, but she didn't say anything, so I went on.

"It's like that's the logical conclusion for how Nick sees the world. Murder. If you believe in your heart that there really is no meaning in the world, that the only interaction that's real is controlling other people, then it's OK to kill someone 'cause it doesn't actually mean anything. Maybe it's even the ultimate form of establishing your dominance and control."

I sucked in a breath and sighed.

"I don't know. If that's what's pouring out of my subconscious mind while I sleep, can I claim to be better than Nick or the bullies at school or anyone else? Are we all just coded to strive for control?"

"I don't think so," she said, her eyes danced along the wall. I don't think she wanted to look at me. "It's just a dream. And you can always change yourself. I was bulimic for a long time, and I'm changing that. Now maybe you found something ugly in yourself that you want to change, too."

I nodded. In a way, she was right, I guess.

"I mean, would you rather just be oblivious to it?" she said. "A lot of people have almost no self-awareness at all."

"It wasn't just the dreams, either, though," I said. "It was exciting to crawl into people's windows and pick through their belongings. I felt free. And awake. Alive. I liked it."

"I'm sure it was…" she trailed off as she reached for the right word. "Stimulating. But I don't know that seeking out the most stimulation possible is a healthy way to live."

"You're right," I said. I was quiet for a long time while I thought it over.

"Still, it's more than that, too, though," I said. "I mean, I kind of trapped you down here in a cage. I didn't think of it that way before, but that's what it is."

"In a way," she said. "But once you realized that, you wanted to change it right? And to talk about it. Communicating is like the opposite of trying to control someone, isn't it?"

She finally looked at me and smiled, and I could see in her eyes that we were connected, not like we were in love or anything, but we were together, and it was real.

"I killed him," I said. "Nick, I mean. He attacked me. Was strangling me. So I fought back. Stabbed him in the neck. Self-defense, you know."

And all of a sudden, I burst into tears. I tried to cover my face, but my mouth sprang open and emitted strange and muted sobs and gasps. Tears and snot flowed down my face like rain on a windshield.

'Cause I knew now that Nick was so wrong. All these things do have meaning. Even a life as bad as his has meaning. And it reminded me of that thing he said about how we only have so many years. In a way that's exactly what gives it meaning. The people you know, and how it can't be forever. Out of the billions of years the Earth has existed, Nick was here for 24 and Tammie for just 19. Now they're gone. I knew them, but if you didn't, it's too late now. It will never happen again.

I leaned back against the cinder blocks and tried to angle myself away from Beth.

The meaning was so big, and the feelings in me got so big, that I sort of convulsed periodically from being overwhelmed. Like I was fighting it. Like if my muscles spasmed just right, I could regain control of myself and stop crying or something.

Beth moved to me and put a hand on my shoulder and rubbed my chest with the other.

"You're OK," she said. "It's going to be OK."

She just kept rubbing my chest, and I think something about that made it even harder to stop crying.

I think your brain does that with your companions. It carves out a spot in your imagination for them to sit, and you can feel them there all the time. And now that they're gone, there's a hole there. An empty space that I can feel always. It's almost like a physical feeling, I mean. Like the universe doesn't feel quite right.

"Let's go home, Jake," she said.

I felt like I could exhale. And I knew we could go home now. And I knew that I could tell her about everything that happened with Nick. All the details. Someday.

We sat in the vacant basement a moment longer, and I had this weird feeling, knowing that the old me would've been too scared. Would've froze. Would've hid these things from her forever. I don't know how we ever would've gotten out of this room.

I guess she was right.

You can change yourself.

CHAPTER 33

IT'S BEEN A LONG TIME since I've written in here. Six or eight weeks, I guess. I didn't feel like obsessing about myself on paper anymore, so I stopped for a while.

Don't worry. I kept busy.

Winter came along and dumped thirteen inches of snow on everything tonight. The wind roared. The tree branches shivered. Plow trucks scraped by, their yellow lights circling over everything, but they couldn't keep up. The fat flakes plunged to the ground faster than they could bulldoze them clear.

All of the people ran to hide, huddling around heating vents and fireplaces and wood burning stoves. The streets emptied. The businesses closed early.

After many hours, the snow finally stopped, and the wind died down, but the temperature plummeted. The slushy stuff that plows and shovels and salt had stirred up now hardened into thick sheets of ice. The cold gripped everything and held it still.

The weather guy on TV warned it was "dicey" out there. He cautioned to only go out in an emergency.

But I couldn't sleep, so I went out at 2:46 am to trudge around in it for a while anyway.

The streets were empty. No cars. No pedestrians. No birds. No movement at all. The wind died down now that the storm had moved on, and everything stood motionless.

The snow deadened the noise even more like those foam sheets they hang in the room where the marching band practices at school. It killed all the reverberations in a way that made the silence seem closer and dryer than usual, like it was right on top of me. I fought back a little with the crunch and squeak of my walking.

A bank sign caked with snow glowed faintly red from the concealed light within. I kicked my way through powdery white stuff and thought back on how it all went down.

It had only been a few months since all of this started. In some ways it seemed like it was just a few days, and in other ways it felt like forever ago that I first hung out at Nick and Donnie's apartment and heard stories about bridge shitting and dead bodies and sour cream guns. Did I have more perspective with the passing of time? Maybe.

I started out thinking about Beth. She and I are still friends, and I know now that it's all we can ever be. The whole basement thing changed things between us. In a weird way, I think it might have made us closer. (I mean, a man and a woman share a certain bond once he's locked her in a confined space for an extended period, right? OK not really.) It's a different kind of close, though. Like people who went through something fucked up together and now have deep yet mixed feelings about each other. A close with damage that can never be repaired.

Don't take that the wrong way, though. She still means a lot to me. I guess I just don't idealize her the way I used to, and in turn she is definitely a little more closed off to me or something, which I can understand.

Like I passed her in the hall at school today, and I think she probably saw me, but she kept talking to Nikki Turner like she didn't.

That's fine, really. I mean, not only do I empathize with her point of view, I'm almost embarrassed when I think back to the crush I had on her in the first place. Not 'cause of anything about her so much as how naive I was about everything for so long.

I guess every dumb kid probably endures a crush on some girl that seems unattainable. Maybe if they all got a little closer, they'd see that most of it was in their imagination. Like I said, there's nothing wrong with Beth. She's a good person and all that, but I can see now that I was in love with the idea of "winning" a person, not in love with an actual person.

In any case, I am thankful as hell that she decided to lie to her parents about the basement stuff. She told them she ran away to a friend's house. I guess they were so happy that she was home and safe and all of that, they didn't really feel the need to dig all that deeply, or if they did, she found some way to shut it down, I guess. I owe her for that.

I inhaled too deeply and felt the sharp pain of the cold taking hold deep within my nose. It felt like the skin in my nostrils was cracking. I stopped and slipped my gloves off to rub at it for a second, and the silence enveloped me again. After a second I heard the plow grinding along somewhere in the distance.

I've been working on a bunch of shit, though. I write 2,000 words every day to try to wire that skill into my brain. I don't know if obsessively writing about yourself in a journal helps you that much in the long run, so I've written fiction instead. Dialogue, mostly. That's what I want to get good at. I think my writing mostly sucks for now, but I'm a long way from putting in my 10,000 hours, so that's OK. I will get there.

I started making myself read at least 100 pages a day as well. I figure that's wiring some shit, too. And it's a good habit.

I also do this high-intensity interval training now on this old exercise bike in the basement of our apartment building. It's this crazy exercise routine where you do a balls-out sprint for one minute and then cool down for three minutes and repeat a few times. I guess sprinting like that is way more effective than the typical low-intensity workout like jogging or whatever. It kicks your metabolism up for days at a time and floods your brain with endorphins and stuff. Sweat pours from everywhere, and I feel sick about twenty seconds into the first sprint, but if I power through the pain of the first ten minutes, this rush comes over me and lasts for the rest of the day. I feel warm all over and have all of this energy.

It's funny 'cause I'm not even into all that vanity workout bullshit. I don't care what I look like. I sure as shit am not going to post pictures of my shirtless self on Instagram to show my progress or anything like that. I think we can all agree that those people are the worst. I just think we weren't designed to be sedentary is all. It's better for my mind to get some exercise along with the cardiovascular benefits, and it's always better to start right now.

That's the thing, man. Whatever ideas I get, whatever I think I might want to achieve, I fucking go get it. Immediately. I used to spend all my time obsessing about the things that were seemingly out of my control and wondering what these things meant about me. Like all I could do was watch what happened to me and wonder who that made me. I felt destined to merely observe life. But I realize now that there are things I can control, a bunch of them, and that's where all of my attention goes. Life is way too fucking short, so leap straight for the goddamn jugular while you've got the chance, I say.

I stomped through a little wooded area by the tennis courts behind the school. A row of pine trees to my right slumped under the weight of the snow. I thought about giving one a shake, but I decided I was too cold for such nonsense and kept moving.

Even when I look back on what happened with Nick, there's a sadness to it, but it's out of my control now, so I don't concern myself with it much. I got that weepy bullshit out of my system in the basement, thankfully, and just moved on. I just let it go like a little kid watching his balloon float upward and forever out of view.

The cold dried out my skin now as I lifted my feet to march past Nick's apartment. I thought maybe Donnie would be there playing video games, but all the lights were off. I guess maybe he moved away after everything that happened.

A construction crew found the bodies in the partially excavated foundation they were working on a few blocks from there. I don't know if Nick thought they were filling it in, and he could just sneak the bodies in, and no one would take note or what. I guess maybe when you have to hide four bodies at a moment's notice, you don't have a lot of time to think of the long term.

Aside from Tammie, they identified two others. A husband and wife in their fifties. The cops think they probably interrupted Nick during one of his burglaries. Because of course they found tons of stolen loot in his apartment along with $27,000 cash hidden under the floorboards. One of the things they found was an opal and diamond ring that belonged to the dead woman.

The other body is a younger girl. Or I guess I should say "was" a younger girl. They think twenties or thirties. But they don't know her name. Jane Doe. She was rotted worse than the others, so they tried to identify her via dental records, but so far have come up empty.

The cold hardened the top layer of snow, so my steps packed more of a crunch than before. My cheeks hurt, and when I licked my lips, they felt all dry and cracked like lizard skin or something.

I still puzzle over Nick's view of the world. My mind tumbles and spins all the things he said over and over like a washing machine I can't turn off. I know he was wrong, but maybe there was some kernel of truth in there somewhere. Or, if not truth, at least something important.

I don't know.

I look for meaning even though I know I won't really find it. I do it because I have no choice, I think. I can see the meaning in something like Tammie's death, in that she was a unique individual that is gone forever. But that doesn't really give me meaning going forward in my own life — not all the way, at least. It doesn't give me a direction or a goal or fulfillment or anything like that.

But I look for meaning anyway. I look for it in books. I look for it in relationships. I look for it in the endless crowds of kids funneling in and out of the school. I look for it in death. I look for it in the snow in the middle of the night while the rest of the world sleeps. I look for it goddamn everywhere.

Casting Shadows Everywhere

I look for meaning because I'm still here.

CHAPTER 34

HOLY FUCK, DUDE. YOU ARE not going to believe this. I hope, as a matter of fact, that you're sitting down right now. (For the sake of your own physical well being, of course.)

The McRib is back.

Yes, you read that correctly. (Of course, if you weren't sitting, you probably just fainted and bashed your damn head in. Idiot! I told you to sit the hell down.) The most delicious sandwich on Earth is back for a limited time. I just pounded down two of these sons-a-bitches. Smeared BBQ sauce frickin' everywhere. And believe you me, I was loving every minute of it. Yep. These little motherfuckers are tasty as hell.

♦　　♦　　♦

Wow. I should probably burn this journal.

AUTHOR'S NOTE

Thanks for reading the 2019 edition of Casting Shadows Everywhere. We'd greatly appreciate if you took a moment to review the book on Amazon.

This book has taken quite a journey to find its way to your hands.

This was our first novel, completed way back in the summer of 2012. Jake's journey has gone through a lot of drafts over the years, including a big revamp in 2019.

What's different about the 2019 version? Well, we added about 5,000 words of all-new material, rewrote a few chunks, moved some things around, and got out our trusty scalpels with which we sliced it up pretty good, stabbing all the bad parts until they died.

This is the definitive director's cut. All the shadows have finally been cast exactly as we want them, and I'm very pleased with it.

It was actually a lot of fun to go back to this one, like visiting an old friend in the mental hospital. Casting Shadows Everywhere is a unique book. (I could say weird, but I'll go with unique.) The story both charms and creeps me out. I suppose that makes it a pretty good expression of what I like about fiction and art in general. I'm proud of it.

Back when we first sent this novel to agents, one of them told us it was "objectionable content" and that their agency would have no interest in something like it. As it happens, that agent no longer works in the publishing industry, but Casting Shadows Everywhere still does. Thousands of people have read it now, and new readers find it every day.

Bottom line: that agent can suck it.

-Tim & LT
Kalamazoo, Michigan
March 7th, 2019

COME PARTY WITH US

We're loners. Rebels. But much to our surprise, the most kickass part of writing has been connecting with our readers. From time to time, we send out newsletters with giveaways, special offers, and juicy details on new releases.

Sign up for our mailing list at:
http://ltvargus.com/mailing-list

ABOUT THE AUTHORS

Tim McBain writes because life is short, and he wants to make something awesome before he dies. Additionally, he likes to move it, move it.

You can connect with Tim via email at tim@timmcbain.com.

L.T. Vargus grew up in Hell, Michigan, which is a lot smaller, quieter, and less fiery than one might imagine. When not click-clacking away at the keyboard, she can be found sewing, fantasizing about food, and rotting her brain in front of the TV.

If you want to wax poetic about pizza or cats, you can contact L.T. (the L is for Lex) at ltvargus9@gmail.com or on Twitter @ltvargus.

LTVargus.com